Prai

"The setting is perfect, the characters are complex and endearing, making this story a heartwarming journey. Hard to say goodbye."
—*Goodreads* review on *Meant for Each Other*

"A warmhearted journey from loss and guilt to self-forgiveness and love."
—*Romantic Times Book Reviews* on *Once Upon Nantucket*

"Complex characters, wonderful seaside setting, and a heartwarming plot make this story hard to put down."
—*Goodreads* review on *The Hero Next Door*

"A wonderful story of forgiveness and healing and second chances…and don't we all need to be swept away in this day and time to be reminded how great it is to love and be loved. You can't go wrong with a book from Irene Hannon."
—*Amazon* review on *A Father for Zach*

"Inspiring prose and embraceable characters…capture the reader from the very first pages."
—*New York Journal of Books* on *That Certain Summer*

"Hannon's multithread plot is woven beautifully together to create a tapestry that will enchant romantics of all ages."
—*Publishers Weekly* on *One Perfect Spring*

"A great summer read…relatable characters with real-life problems."
—*Radiant Lit* on *Seaside Reunion*

Meant for Each Other

Lighthouse Lane—Book Three
Encore Edition

IRENE HANNON

©2010 by Irene Hannon
First edition published 2010 by Harlequin Love Inspired as *The Doctor's Perfect Match*
Encore Edition published 2023 by Irene Hannon
(An Encore Edition is a previously published novel that has been re-edited and reissued with a new cover.)

All rights reserved. No part of this publication may be reproduced, stored in a retrieval system, or transmitted in any form or by any means—for example, electronic, photocopy, recording—without the prior written permission of the author. The only exception is brief quotations in printed reviews.

ISBN 9781970116182

This book is a work of fiction. Names, characters, places, and incidents are the product of the author's imagination or are used fictitiously. Any resemblance to actual events, locales, or persons, living or dead, is coincidental.

To Jo Ann Case—
My forever young friend.
Happy 90th birthday!

1

The woman was crying.

From a tucked-away table in his favorite Nantucket eatery, Christopher Morgan gave the blonde a discreet scrutiny over the rim of his coffee cup.

Even without the tears—and despite her dim corner booth—that pinup figure and flaxen hair would be hard to miss.

Yet all the other patrons of the popular restaurant seemed oblivious to her—and her distress. They were too focused on their companions.

He, on the other hand, was alone.

As was the woman.

His gaze swung back to her as she turned away from her bowl of half-eaten chowder to rummage in her purse, the sheen on her cheeks mute testimony to her misery.

Frowning, Christopher set his cup back on the saucer, fighting his natural inclination to go to her aid. It wasn't wise to offer assistance to strangers these days. Magnanimous gestures could arouse resentment, suspicion—or worse.

And as he'd learned to his regret, crying women were a disaster waiting to happen. The safest course was to steer a wide berth around them.

Besides, after his busy shift in the ER, tiptoeing through the minefield the blonde no doubt represented would be too taxing on his waning energy.

As he sipped his coffee, she dabbed away the evidence of her tears with a tissue, tucked it back in her purse, and withdrew a ten-dollar bill. After laying it on the table, she scooted to the edge of the booth and swiveled on the seat.

The clingy fabric of her black cocktail dress inched up, revealing a stellar pair of legs.

His gaze got stuck there.

All at once, the woman rose and yanked her skirt down until the hem brushed the top of her knees.

He shifted his focus to her face.

She was glaring at him, the color high in her cheeks as she tugged at a modest neckline below a single strand of pearls.

Heat crept up his neck. He was *not* a voyeur, despite her obvious indignation.

But as their gazes locked for a brief moment, it wasn't outrage that contorted her features. It was distress…and defeat. She also seemed on the verge of tears again.

Before he could process her reaction, she circled the room in the opposite direction to avoid passing his table and disappeared out the door.

So much for his attempt to chill out after a long day.

He sighed, finished his coffee in two swigs, and settled his bill. No sense lingering. His relaxing dinner was a bust.

Outside, he picked up his pace as he strode toward his car under the dark clouds that had replaced the bright, sunny skies of earlier in the day. A steady drizzle had also begun to fall, compelling the strollers and sightseers to seek refuge in the shops and restaurants that lined the streets in the heart of the old town.

All except one.

As he drove up Main Street, the woman from the restaurant was trudging through the rain.

She didn't have an umbrella—yet she wasn't hurrying. Nor

did she seem to be paying any attention to her surroundings.

A conclusion verified a moment later when she stumbled in her high heels on the uneven brick sidewalk.

Christopher pressed on the brake, slowing his forward momentum. Walking around Nantucket in shoes like that was an accident waiting to happen, as all his colleagues could attest. Dozens of women who'd chosen fashion over comfort showed up with sprains every year in the ER.

But she righted herself and moved on.

As he approached his turnoff to Orange Street, she continued on Main, her shoulders slumped. She paid no attention to the low rumble of thunder that reverberated through the still air or the flash of lightning that zigzagged across the sky in the distance.

She was either oblivious to the storm—or didn't care about the danger.

Both scenarios were disturbing.

He watched as she veered left on Fair Street and disappeared from view, the story of the Good Samaritan echoing in his mind. Like the traveler to Jericho, this woman seemed in need of a helping hand.

But so had Denise.

Decision made.

Christopher turned left onto Orange Street and accelerated toward 'Sconset.

The troubled blonde wasn't his problem. The smart course was to put as much distance as possible between them.

Even if the image of her defeated eyes refused to be expunged.

* * *

"Are you getting a cold, dear?"

Stifling a sneeze, Marci Clay continued to wash the china plates by hand as Edith Shaw bustled in from The Devon Rose's dining room with another tray of glasses.

"I hope not."

"You've been working too hard since you've been here." Her new sister-in-law's Lighthouse Lane neighbor tut-tutted as she slid the tray onto the stainless-steel prep station in the middle of the kitchen. "Your offer to manage the tearoom while Heather and JC are on their honeymoon was very generous, but you have to be tired. *I* am—especially after yesterday afternoon's birthday party. I thought the guests would never leave."

Hard to argue with that—but given her meager cash reserves, it had been the best wedding gift she'd been able to offer. And with her just-earned diploma in hand and no job yet lined up, she had the time.

But her assumption that years of waitressing experience would be sufficient for The Devon Rose had been way too optimistic—a fact she'd quickly realized during last week's indoctrination under Heather's tutelage. The world of high tea and Ronnie's Diner were at opposite ends of the dining spectrum.

Edith's willingness to help had been the saving grace—plus the invaluable support of Heather's capable assistant, Julie Watson. With those two women to back her up, the job had seemed doable.

Until she got the sniffles.

"Having a few second thoughts?" Edith gave her a keen perusal. Despite her gray hair, the woman radiated youthful energy—and acumen.

"Maybe." She shoved aside a springy curl with the back of her wet hand. "I feel a bit out of my league among all this linen and fine china and sterling silver."

"Join the club." Edith planted her hands on her ample hips. "I'm more of a chili-dog-and-French-fry gal myself. And I'm sure Emily Post or Miss Manners would have a field day critiquing my table etiquette. But if I can get the hang of this tea thing, you can too."

"I appreciate the encouragement." The words came out scratchy as Marci continued to work through the pile of plates.

"Goodness!" Edith peered at her. "I hate to say it, but that sounds like the beginning of a cold to me."

"I think it's fatigue."

That was possible. After all, working extra hours at Ronnie's to build up her anemic savings account, staying up late and consuming far too much caffeine studying for finals and finishing term papers, then rushing off to Nantucket to learn the ropes at The Devon Rose and participate in all the wedding festivities had taken a toll.

The walk home in the rain last night from the restaurant hadn't helped, either.

Why, oh why, had she indulged in that pity party? Letting regrets about her own bad choices overshadow her joy in JC's well-deserved happiness had been foolish.

"I'll tell you what." Edith surveyed the kitchen. "We've got most of the mess cleaned up. The tearoom's closed tomorrow and Tuesday, so there's nothing urgent that needs to be done today. Why don't you turn in and let me finish up? It's better to throw off a cold early than to run yourself down and end up sicker."

That didn't seem fair to the older woman—but she *was* feeling more lethargic by the minute.

"If you're sure you don't mind, I think I'll take you up on that offer."

"Of course I don't mind." Edith shooed her away from the

sink and pushed up the sleeves of her I ♥ Nantucket sweatshirt. "Heather's been like a daughter to me. With her married to JC now, that makes you family—and families help each other."

Not always.

The only one in their family who'd done any helping was JC. The man was a saint for sticking by her and Nathan through the dark times, despite their efforts to push him away. Thankfully, they'd both gotten their acts together—but they had a lot to make up for on the one-for-all, all-for-one front.

Another reason she was determined to follow through on her commitment to keep The Devon Rose running during the honeymoon.

She could *not* get sick.

"Thanks again, Edith."

"Not a problem. Get upstairs and go to bed."

She didn't argue.

And as she crawled under the covers five minutes later, she sent a strong eviction notice to whatever bug was trying to establish a toehold inside her tired body.

* * *

"Thanks for stopping by, Christopher. Sorry to interrupt your holiday weekend."

Christopher frowned as he followed Edith to the front door of her house.

Holiday weekend?

Oh. Right. This was Memorial Day. Most people were probably eating barbecue, visiting with family, or enjoying the beach.

For him, it was just another workday.

"No worries, Edith. I had to come into town anyway to see a

few patients in the hospital—and I'm on duty in the ER later."

"Don't you ever take a day off?"

"Now and then."

She stopped at the door, her hand on the knob. "You know what they say about all work and no play."

"I'll keep that in mind."

"You do that. Anyway, I hated to call you, but Kate frets so much about Maddie that I get paranoid over even the slightest sniffle when I'm babysitting the girls."

"It's safer to err on the side of caution with asthma. I'm glad it was a false alarm." Unlike a few others on his numerous trips to the small cottage tucked between Edith's house and The Devon Rose that the charter fishing captain and her husband called home.

"Me too."

"Well…" Christopher shifted his black medical bag from one hand to the other and tapped his watch. "The ER awaits."

Twin furrows appeared on Edith's brow. "I hate to delay you any further, but I'm also concerned about Heather's new sister-in-law."

"Heather Anderson? From The Devon Rose?" He motioned toward the tearoom.

"Yes."

"She got married this weekend, didn't she? I think I saw an announcement in the church bulletin."

"Yes. A small, intimate wedding. Very romantic."

"What's the problem with her sister-in-law?"

"I hope nothing. She's supposed to manage the tearoom while Heather and JC are in Europe on their honeymoon, but yesterday she seemed to be getting sick. If she's still feeling under the weather, would you mind popping in before you go to the hospital? I could rustle up a loaf of pumpkin bread for you to sweeten the deal."

Christopher hitched up one side of his mouth. "Sold."

"Give me one minute while I phone her." She waved him to a chair and disappeared toward the back of the house.

The minute stretched to five, and when Edith returned with a plastic-wrapped loaf of pumpkin bread in hand, her face was etched with concern. "She sounds terrible—but she said asking you to stop by is too much of an imposition and not to bother."

"As you pointed out, I'm here anyway. It's no bother." Christopher picked up his bag.

"I couldn't convince her of that. But between you and me, I think her reluctance may be more related to finances than inconvenience. According to JC, she's been pinching pennies to put herself through school. Plus, she may not have much, if any, insurance."

"I'm running a special today. Buy one house call, get one free." He winked at Edith. "At least that will be my story when I show up at her door. What's her name?"

"Marci Clay. She's a charming woman. Pretty too. I'm surprised she's not married." Edith twisted the knob and moved aside to allow him to pass. "Maybe she'll meet someone on Nantucket."

"That could happen, I suppose." He stepped out onto the porch.

"I wouldn't be at all surprised."

At the curious nuance in her inflection, Christopher angled back—but her expression was guileless.

His imagination must be working overtime.

"Call me if you have any more concerns about Maddie."

"I'll do that. But at the moment, I'm more worried about Marci."

"I'll check her out."

Edith handed him the pumpkin bread. "Sounds like a plan. Enjoy the treat."

She closed the door with a soft click—but not before he caught a suspicious gleam in her eyes.

And that was *not* his imagination.

Edith was trying to set him up.

But that was a lost cause. No matter how charming or how pretty Marci Clay was, he wasn't interested.

Maybe someday he'd test the waters of romance again. Maybe.

But after steering clear of all eligible women during his two years living on Nantucket, a course change wasn't in his plans for the foreseeable future.

No matter how hard Edith might push.

* * *

As the doorbell chimed—again—Marci groaned and rolled toward the window. First a call from Edith, now this.

Judging by the angle of the sun slanting through the sheer curtains, it was too early for visitors.

Except this one didn't seem to realize that. Nor did her persistent caller appear to have any intention of going away.

Heaving a sigh, she swung her legs to the floor and reached for the ratty velour bathrobe that had wrapped her in its fleecy warmth and comforted her through many a cold, lonely Chicago evening. After shrugging into it, she shuffled down the hall on unsteady legs, clinging to the banister as she descended the stairs.

Whoever had parked a finger against the doorbell was about to get an earful—if she could coax any words past her sore throat.

It couldn't feel any more raw if someone had taken sandpaper to it.

At the door, she flipped the deadbolt, twisted the knob, and opened her mouth to give her visitor a piece of her mind.

But her voice deserted her as she came face-to-face with a tall, thirtyish man holding a black bag.

It was the preppy guy from the restaurant who'd been watching her.

She snapped her jaw shut and stared at him.

He stared back.

When the silence lengthened, he swallowed. "Marci Clay?"

She gave a tiny nod.

"I'm Christopher Morgan. Edith asked me to stop by and...uh...check you out." His face reddened a few shades. "She said you weren't feeling well."

The guy who'd ogled her legs was the doctor Edith had offered to send over?

Marci edged back. "I'm fine." She tightened her grip on the door and started to ease it closed. No way did she want this jerk anywhere near her.

"You don't look fine."

Given how she felt, that was likely the understatement of the century.

"I asked Edith to tell you not to bother." The words scraped against her throat.

"And I told her this was your lucky day. Two house calls for the price of one. You can't pass up a bargain like that."

"No one does house calls anymore. Especially for free."

"I do—on occasion. What's your temperature?"

"I have no idea. If there's a thermometer in the house, I haven't found it."

"I have a disposable one in my bag."

Marci dipped her chin and studied the thin blue stripes in his white dress shirt. The thought of getting up close and personal with this guy held zero appeal—but if she wanted to fulfill her obligations at The Devon Rose she needed medical attention. And in light of her shaky finances and bare-bones health insurance, free was hard to pass up.

"Listen...about Saturday night. I'm sorry I stared."

At the unexpected apology, she gave him a quick assessment—and noticed a few features she'd missed on Saturday. Eyes as blue as the Nantucket sea on a sunny day. Shoulders broad enough to carry the heaviest of loads. A firm chin that conveyed strength and resolve. Light brown hair sprinkled with the merest hint of silver at the temples. A kind demeanor that spoke of caring and compassion.

Her attitude softened a fraction.

"I want you to know I'm not that rude as a rule." His steady gaze held hers. "My mother raised me to treat women with respect, and I didn't do that Saturday night. Please forgive me."

Was this guy for real?

Marci scrutinized him for any sign of deceit, any indication that this was a standard line. Like all the others she'd heard in her life.

But unless this guy was a world-class actor, he meant what he'd said. He truly was sorry. And he hadn't been too proud or arrogant or conceited to admit his mistake.

In other words, he was a gentleman.

Not a species she'd often run across in her world.

So how was she supposed to respond?

Her experience tossing sassy comebacks at guys who flirted with her at Ronnie's, where she often spent as much of her shift deflecting advances as she did taking orders and delivering food, didn't provide any guidance about how to accept apologies from a gentleman.

"Umm...it's okay." Lame—but it was the best she could do.

"No, it's not. So why not let me make amends? I can take your temperature, get a bit of history, try to come up with a diagnosis. Edith tells me you're planning to manage The Devon Rose for the next couple of weeks, and it's obvious you're in no shape to do that right now. Helping get you back on your feet is the least I can do after my faux pas on Saturday."

Clever how he'd positioned his assistance as a favor to *him*. But no matter how he framed it, there had to be a catch. There always was.

She leaned against the edge of the door as a sudden weariness swept over her, trying to prod her sluggish brain into gear.

The man's eyes narrowed, and instead of waiting for her to respond, he took her arm in a firm but gentle grip and eased her back into the spacious foyer. After shutting the door with his shoulder, he led her to a chair beside the steps.

"Hey. I didn't invite you in."

"So call the police. Where can I wash my hands?"

Give it up, Marci. Not every guy has a one-track mind—and you do *need help.*

Instead of engaging her painful vocal cords again, she motioned toward the restroom in what had once been the butler's pantry.

As he strode across the hardwood floor and disappeared through the dining room archway, she let her head drop back against the wall beneath the stairs that wound to the second floor.

In general, high-handed men riled her. Yet despite his take-charge manner, Christopher Morgan came across as caring and competent rather than autocratic.

Besides, she couldn't afford to take offense. She needed to get well, and it would be foolish to pass up free medical help.

But if he pulled out a stethoscope and aimed for her chest, he was going to end up with a smack on the cheek—or worse.

* * *

What a weird coincidence.

Christopher twisted the faucet off and dried his hands on one of the disposable guest towels beside the sink.

The odds of crossing paths again with the woman in the restaurant had to be minuscule.

Unless more than chance was involved.

How many coincidences in the past had turned out, in retrospect, to be part of God's plan for him? Too many to count. And this could be one of them.

Perhaps it would be best to go with the flow.

As he returned to the foyer, his shoes silent on the large Chinese area rug in the dining room, Marci came into view. Her head rested against the wall, exposing the slender, delicate column of her throat, and her eyes were closed, the curve of her long lashes sweeping her cheeks in a graceful arc.

His step faltered.

On Saturday, he'd been distracted by her great figure and fabulous legs, but today those assets were camouflaged by a worn, faded pink robe that covered her neck to toes. Instead, he directed his attention to her face. Her halo of blond hair softened a chin that was a tad too sharp, while well-defined cheekbones gave her features a slight angular appearance, adding a dash of character that kept her from being just another Kewpie-doll blonde. Full, appealing lips completed the picture.

In other words, Marci Clay was the kind of woman who would draw any man's attention.

But perhaps not for the right reasons—and her reaction to his appreciative once-over Saturday night indicated she knew that.

Her lashes fluttered, propelling him forward. If she caught him staring again, she'd no doubt hustle him out the door faster than a sand crab could scuttle back to its hole.

That suspicion was confirmed by the wariness in her deep green irises as he approached. While he couldn't help noticing the flecks of gold that sparked in their depths as he pulled up a chair beside her, he did his best to ignore them.

After snapping on a pair of latex gloves, he withdrew a disposable thermometer from his bag and tore off the wrapping. "Open up. We'll have a reading in sixty seconds."

He slid it under her tongue, and as they waited he took her pulse. Strong, if a bit fast. No issues there. The subtle tremors beneath his fingertips were more concerning. They could be due to weakness—but odds were the cause was fever-related chills. Given the heat seeping through his glove, he wasn't going to like her temperature.

At the one-minute mark, he withdrew the thermometer. The number wasn't a surprise. "A hundred and two."

She grimaced.

He slipped it into a small waste bag and gave her his full attention. "Any idea what's going on?"

She shook her head.

"When did this start?"

"Yesterday."

"Anything hurt?"

"Throat."

"Any other symptoms?"

Again she shook her head.

He withdrew a tongue depressor and penlight from his bag. Scooted closer to her. "Let's have a look."

She opened her mouth and he gave her throat a scan. Swelling and severe inflammation. He moved on to gently feel the lymph nodes in her neck. Puffy.

She flinched and tried to pull away. "Hurts."

"Sorry." He let her go and leaned back. "We may be dealing with a case of strep throat."

She squeezed her eyes shut, and her lashes grew spiky with moisture.

"Hey, it's not the end of the world." His reassurance came out soft and husky, and he cleared his throat. That was *not* his usual bedside tone. "You'll be back on your feet in a few days with the right care."

"I don't have a few days." She rasped out the shaky words.

She was worried about her commitment at The Devon Rose.

"We'll get you well as fast as we can. Deal?"

"Wednesday?"

Much as he'd like to say yes, he couldn't lie. "I doubt it."

"When?"

"Why don't we verify the diagnosis first?" He rummaged around in his bag and pulled out a small kit. "This is a rapid strep test. It will give us an answer in a few minutes. I see quite a few pediatric patients in my family practice, so I always have one of these with me. They come in handy, especially for the younger set. Not that you're over the hill, by any means."

His attempt at humor bombed.

Lips flat, she watched him set up the test. "How much?"

It took a moment for her meaning to register.

If she was asking the price of the test, money must be tight—as Edith had implied.

"I get an abundance of free samples. I try to pass that benefit on to my patients." While that was true, this kit wasn't one of them. But she didn't have to know that.

Without giving her a chance to pursue the subject, he instructed her to open her mouth again and proceeded to swipe her throat with a long cotton swab. When he finished, he dipped the swab in a solution and placed a few drops on a test strip.

"While we wait for the results, let's assume it's strep and talk about treatment." He peeled off his gloves and dropped them into the waste bag. "Do you have any medication allergies?"

"No."

"In that case, let's go with penicillin." He started to pull a prescription pad out of his pocket.

"Won't this…" She stopped. Swallowed. Winced. "Won't this go away by itself?"

Money concerns again.

"Yes. It takes three to seven days." Leaving the prescription pad in his pocket, he crossed his arms over his chest.

"Maybe I'll get lucky, and it will be gone in three days." She pulled her robe tighter as a shiver rippled through her.

"That's possible—but antibiotics shorten the contagious period."

"By how much?"

"Most people stop being infectious twenty-four to forty-eight hours after they begin treatment. Without the pills, you could pass germs for two to three weeks, even if your symptoms go away. Not the best scenario in a restaurant." He skimmed the test strip. Flipped it toward her, indicating the test window. "Positive."

Sighing, she pinched the bridge of her nose.

He dropped the strip into the waste bag and sealed the top, scrambling to put together a diplomatic way to offer further assistance. "I'll tell you what. I've got a few samples of penicillin that will get you started." He removed a packet of four pills from his bag and held them out to her.

She didn't take them.

"Thank you—but I doubt that would be enough to kick this bug."

"That's why I'm going to swing by my office on my way back from the hospital later and raid the sample closet. I think I can come up with enough to see you through. That way you won't have to run out to a pharmacy to get a prescription filled and spread germs all over town. I wouldn't want to be responsible for creating a public-health menace." He gave her his most persuasive smile.

Didn't work.

"I'm not in the habit of accepting favors."

Her wary expression explained why.

Other men who'd done favors for her had expected a payback.

A bad taste filled his mouth.

"These come with no strings attached. That's a promise."

She searched his face, and after a few seconds took the pills. "Thank you."

"Do you have any over-the-counter medicine in the house that will help with the fever? Aspirin, ibuprofen?" He rose, bag in hand.

"Yes."

"Take them on a regular basis. Drink extra water. Rest. I'll leave the samples hanging on your doorknob after my shift in the

ER. That way I won't disturb you if you're resting."

He retraced his steps to the door while she trailed behind him. Pausing on the threshold, he withdrew a card from his pocket and handed it to her. "If you feel worse, or the symptoms don't improve by tomorrow, call me."

A few seconds ticked by as she read the card...then lifted her chin. "I appreciate your help. I don't know how I would have coped with this otherwise."

Although she had to be eight or nine inches shorter than his six-foot frame, she radiated a quiet strength and dignity that had likely been hard-earned. Unless he was misreading her, Marci Clay was a survivor—despite her air of defeat and distress on Saturday.

But as history had proven, he wasn't all that adept at reading the female psyche...and *misreading* it was a minefield. It was far safer to avoid complicated women altogether.

Easing away, he shifted back into professional mode. "Happy to assist. This is what being a doctor is supposed to be about. Now rest and take your medicine. You should feel much better by tomorrow. And if all goes well, I expect you can be back on the job by Thursday."

Without waiting for her to respond, he descended the porch steps and strode toward Edith's house, where he'd parked his car.

As he set his bag on the backseat, he glanced toward The Devon Rose. The door was closed, but a movement behind the lace curtain that screened the drawing room from the scrutiny of passersby suggested a human presence on the other side. Had Marci been watching him?

The possibility pleased him—for reasons he refused to examine.

After sliding into the driver's seat, he caught a similar

movement behind the sheer curtains at Edith's living-room window.

Did the older woman have him under surveillance too?

Considering the gleam in her eye earlier, that was an unsettling thought. Edith Shaw was gaining a reputation as a matchmaker, thanks to her part in pairing two couples in the past two years—and he did *not* want to be her next victim.

Even if she had her sights set on a match as lovely as Marci Clay.

2

"The Devon Rose."

"Marci? It's JC."

"JC!" Setting aside a measuring cup, Marci tucked the phone closer to her ear and gave her brother her full attention. "How's Paris?"

"Romantic."

"I'll bet. And how's Heather?"

"Happy. Gorgeous. Irresistible."

A female giggle sounded in the background, followed by a chuckle from JC. It was good to hear her big brother sounding lighthearted. He'd had more than enough worry to last a lifetime.

"Tell her I said hi."

"Will do. How's everything going?"

"No complaints. I'm whipping up a batch of scones from her recipe as we speak."

"I told Heather you'd breeze through. But you know how to reach us if you need us."

While *breeze through* wasn't quite accurate, the penicillin *had* vanquished the strep throat in less than forty-eight hours. She'd let Edith and Julie handle the tearoom today, but now that the last of their Wednesday guests had departed, she felt well enough to do a little baking. And if she continued to improve, she'd be back on the job tomorrow.

"Your itinerary and contact numbers are taped to the fridge.

I read them every morning so I can live your European tour vicariously. That's probably the closest I'll ever get to the real thing."

"Hey—your turn will come."

Not likely. That kind of happy ending wasn't in the cards for a woman like her.

Nevertheless, she tried to lighten her tone. "Anything is possible, I suppose."

"It is—with God."

"He and I aren't well-acquainted."

"You could be."

Outside the window, a bird took flight and aimed for the sky. JC's faith was admirable—but it wasn't for her. "You never give up, do you?"

"No. And my persistence paid off with Nathan."

"That was different. Trust me. I'm a lost cause." The swinging door from the dining room opened as Edith bustled through with a tray, giving her an excuse to change the subject. "We're in cleanup mode here, so I need to get back to work. Besides, I'm sure you have better things to do on your honeymoon than talk to your sister."

Is that JC? Edith mouthed the question.

She nodded.

"Tell him I said hi. Heather too."

Marci relayed the message.

"I'll pass that on. Call us if you need us."

"I will. Don't worry about anything here. Focus on having fun."

"We intend to. Talk to you soon."

As the line went dead, Marci set the portable phone back in its holder on the counter and picked up the measuring cup.

Edith planted her hands on her hips. "Don't I get a report?"

"I didn't ask for details." Marci filled the cup with flour and leveled it off. "But I got the impression they're enjoying themselves. And JC sounds happy."

The older woman's lips curved up. "Excellent. I knew from day one those two would be a perfect match. But getting them to see that took a bit of work."

Marci had heard all about Edith's penchant for matchmaking. Although Heather claimed her neighbor's efforts hadn't had that much impact on her relationship with JC, it was obvious Edith felt otherwise. Why disillusion her?

"All I know is I'm grateful they met. I'd given up on JC ever finding a wife."

"It was just a matter of meeting the right woman. Or, in Heather's case, the right man." Edith began emptying the tray. "And speaking of men…is there some handsome man pining away for you back in Chicago?"

The only one missing her in Chicago was Ronnie at the diner—and by no stretch of the imagination could the fifty-something cook with the receding hairline and prominent paunch be called handsome.

"No. Men are more trouble than they're worth." She dumped the flour into a mixing bowl.

"Goodness. That's exactly what Heather used to say. Until JC came along, that is." The older woman picked up the empty tray and bustled back toward the dining room, pausing on the threshold. "By the way, I saw Christopher Morgan at a meeting at church last night. He asked how you were doing. He's single, you know."

With a wink, Edith pushed through the swinging door and disappeared.

Marci stared after her. Was Edith hinting that the doctor was interested in her? That the two of them—

No.

She cut off that preposterous line of thought. They knew nothing about each other. Meaning that if the man *was* interested in her, it was for the wrong reasons—and hormones were no basis for a relationship. Been there, done that…and repeating the experience held no appeal.

But she did owe him a thank-you for his visit on Monday. Without his intervention, she'd still be out of commission. Would a note suffice?

Somehow that didn't seem quite adequate.

Perhaps a small token of appreciation?

As she gathered the dough together with a few quick kneads, dropped it onto the floured counter, and began rolling and cutting out the scones, inspiration struck. Food. What man didn't like home-cooked food? Her killer chocolate-chip-pecan cookies would do the trick…except that seemed a bit personal.

Why not send him a gift certificate for the tearoom? He could even bring a date if he wanted to.

Perfect.

As she slid the baking sheet of scones into the oven, Edith returned to the kitchen.

"Julie's almost finished refilling the sugar bowls." The older woman set another tray of plates on the counter and moved toward the refrigerator. "I'll work on the jam and clotted cream for tomorrow. Another full house, according to the reservation book."

"Thanks. I like the idea of getting a jump on tomorrow's prep."

Marci considered the woman as Edith got to work. She might know Christopher Morgan's home address. According to

Heather, the older woman was well-connected on the island. Even though she and Chester weren't natives, they'd embraced island life after their move to Nantucket a dozen years ago following his retirement.

But in light of Edith's implication that the man was interested in her—and the Lighthouse Lane matriarch's penchant for arranging romantic pairings—that could be a tactical error. The proximity of her living arrangements once JC returned didn't help, either. It had been generous of her brother to rent the cottage behind Edith's house for her during her month-long vacation, but dodging matchmaking attempts would be awkward...and stressful

It would be far safer to find the kindhearted doctor's address on her own, take care of the thank-you that etiquette demanded—and do her best to forget they'd ever met.

* * *

Christopher leaned his bike against the wall of his tiny 'Sconset cottage and shuffled through his mail as he walked to the back door, feet crunching on the oystershell path. Bill, bill, ad, postcard from Bermuda—he flipped it over and skimmed the message from his brother...along with the happy face at the bottom, courtesy of his seven-year-old nephew.

"Hey there, Christopher." His landlord raised a hand in greeting from the other side of the picket fence that separated the yards of their adjoining cottages, which backed to the sea.

"Hi, Henry. What's up?" He strolled over, giving the older man a swift assessment.

"Now, you put away those doctor eyes of yours." The man shook a finger at him. "Don't be sizing me up every time we talk just because I had a bout of pneumonia last winter. I hope you're as resilient as I am at eighty-four."

"I do too." That was the truth. In the past two years, since he'd rented Henry's second, tiny cottage, the man had bounced back from the few ailments he'd experienced.

"Any exciting mail?"

At Henry's question, Christopher riffled through the letters again. "Bills and ads for the most part—but I did get a postcard from my brother." He handed it over.

His neighbor pulled a pair of wire-rimmed glasses from his shirt pocket, settled them on his nose, and examined the photo of the expansive beach. "Pretty, isn't it? Always wanted to see that pink sand." He extended it over the fence.

"Would you still like to go?"

"Nope. After all the gallivanting I did in my Army days, I'm happy to be an armchair traveler now. Don't have to worry about terrorists on airplanes or fighting crowds or losing luggage. You can't beat the Travel Channel." He leaned closer to Christopher and peered at one of the envelopes in his hand. "That looks interesting."

Christopher scanned the return address. The Devon Rose.

Huh.

He slit the envelope and pulled out a single sheet of paper folded in half. Inside he found a gift certificate and a short note written in a scrawling hand.

Dr. Morgan:

Thank you for your assistance on Monday. The penicillin took care of the problem. Please enjoy tea for two as a token of my appreciation.

It was signed by Marci Clay.

The message was about as impersonal as you could get—yet

Christopher's heart warmed as he ran a finger over the words inked by Marci's hand.

"Maybe interesting wasn't the right word."

At Henry's speculative appraisal, heat crept up Christopher's neck. "It's a gift certificate. I did an impromptu house call a few days ago, and the patient was grateful." He waved the envelope at Henry and changed the subject. "You ever been here?"

His diversionary tactic didn't work.

"Female patient?"

Despite his age, the man was still razor-sharp—and if he tried to dodge the question, Henry would get more suspicious.

"Yes. Her brother just married the owner, and she's running the place while they're on their honeymoon." Christopher fingered the gift certificate as an idea took shape. "Don't you have a birthday coming up?"

"I stopped counting those long ago."

"June eighth." Henry might pretend not to care about his birthday, but he'd been thrilled last year with an invitation for dinner at the upscale Chanticleer. "Why don't you and I give this a try on your big day?" He held up the gift certificate.

Sliding his palms into the back pockets of his slacks, Henry bowed forward like a reed, knobby elbows akimbo, expression dubious. "Kind of fancy-schmancy, isn't it?"

"You deserve fancy on your birthday."

"You ought to take some pretty little lady to a place like that."

An image of Marci flashed through his mind, but Christopher pushed it aside. "Pretty little ladies seem to be in short supply these days."

"You're not looking in the right places, then."

"I'm not looking, period."

"I know." Henry sighed. "But you've got to move on,

Christopher. You can't let one painful experience ruin your life. I learned that after Korea. There were guys in my outfit who couldn't get past the bad stuff once they came home. Haunted them for the rest of their lives. I wouldn't want that to happen to you. You're thirty-six years old. You should have a wife and a bunch of kids by now."

"I'll get around to that one of these days."

"You said that last year."

Christopher laid a hand on the older man's bony shoulder. "I appreciate your concern, Henry. But this is best for now." He lifted the certificate again. "In the meantime, do we have a date?"

After a few moments, a slow grin split his face. "I expect we do. Shall I break out my tie?"

"I will if you will."

"It's a deal. And maybe we'll see that female patient of yours while we're there."

That could happen.

But no matter what starry-eyed fantasy Henry's romantic brain might be spinning, the reality was straightforward.

They were going to The Devon Rose to celebrate a birthday. Period.

Even if the thought of seeing Marci Clay again was sending a tiny tingle of anticipation zipping through his veins.

* * *

As Marci returned from showing two guests to their table, a tall man with deep blue eyes, dressed in khaki slacks and a navy blazer, stepped into the foyer of The Devon Rose.

Christopher Morgan.

The fine fan of lines at the corners of his lashes crinkled when he spotted her. "You're looking much improved."

A disconcerting ripple of warmth spread through her as he drew close, and she wiped her palms down her slim black skirt. "I'm *feeling* much improved."

"Glad to hear it." He held up a familiar piece of paper. "I'm here to redeem my gift certificate. I have a reservation."

News to her. Julie must have taken it.

She turned aside to skim the names on the day's seating chart. There it was. Morgan. Table six. For two.

He'd brought a date.

The warmth evaporated.

Pasting on a smile, she angled back.

Instead of the gorgeous female she expected, however, a wiry, wizened older gent with thin, neatly combed gray hair popped out from behind Christopher. He beamed at her, but directed his question to his companion. "Is this the lady who sent you the certificate?"

"She's the one."

The man's grin broadened as he refocused on her. "It's my birthday. Eighty-five years and counting."

"Wow! That does deserve a celebration."

"At my age, every day I wake up is worth celebrating." Eyes twinkling, he stuck out his hand. "Henry Calhoun. I'm Christopher's neighbor. Nice to meet you."

She returned his firm shake. "Marci Clay."

"Swanky place you have here." He perused the foyer and grand staircase. "My wife came here once, years ago. Enjoyed it very much, as I recall."

"We'll do our best to see that you do too."

The front door opened again, admitting more patrons, and Christopher turned to Henry. "We'd better let Ms. Clay show us to our table."

"Maybe she can stop by and chat with us again later."

"I'd be happy to." She led the way to their corner table in one of the twin parlors and offered them a tea menu. "Julie will be back in a few minutes to answer any questions and take your tea order. Enjoy the experience."

"We will. I even wore a tie for the occasion." Henry flapped the out-of-date accessory at her.

Marci tried to mask her amusement. Based on width alone, the tie had to be at least twenty years old. "You look very spiffy."

"Spiffy?" One side of Christopher's mouth rose. "Isn't that kind of an old-fashioned term?"

"Maybe she's an old-fashioned girl." Henry shook out his napkin and settled it in his lap. "And if you ask me, no one's ever come up with a finer compliment than spiffy. Thank you, my dear."

"You're very welcome. I'll be back later to see how you enjoyed the tea."

Marci continued to seat guests, doing her best to ignore the pair of men at the corner table. Once the tea got underway, however, it should be easier to focus. Julie was going to handle the twin sitting rooms while she worked a wedding shower in the dining room on the other side of the foyer. Out of sight and all that.

Except it didn't work.

Images of the blue-eyed doctor kept flashing through her mind. Distracting her. She dropped a pair of silver tongs on the floor. Sloshed hot water onto the white linen as she set down a fresh teapot. Knocked over the sugar bowl, sending cubes tumbling across the starched tablecloth.

Too bad she couldn't blame her fumbling on mere physical attraction. That was easier to deal with than this man's deeper appeal. Since his faux pas in the restaurant, he'd been a total gentleman. He wasn't the first man to notice her legs—or her body.

Nor would he be the last. But he *was* the first to apologize for his rude behavior. And it didn't seem fair to hold one brief lapse against him.

As she lifted the lid on the tea chest so the bride-to-be could make her selection, she peeked over her shoulder. If she leaned back a bit, she could just catch a glimpse of his strong profile as he spoke with Henry, the fragile bone china teacup appearing child-size in his long, lean fingers.

Who was Christopher Morgan? Had he been born on Nantucket? Where did he live? What did he like to do when he wasn't working? Did he have a girlfriend?

Expelling a breath, she turned back to the bride-to-be.

None of those questions mattered—least of all the last one. She wasn't going to be on Nantucket long enough to get to know *anyone*. She was here to rest and relax after seven grueling years of school and work. Then she'd begin her job search and build a future that didn't include slinging hash at Ronnie's—or relying on others to validate her worth.

And she didn't need a man in her life to do that.

Only the two men she trusted to love her for the right reasons would be granted access to her heart going forward—her brothers. She could always count on JC and Nathan.

Yet as she closed the tea chest, she couldn't help wishing there was room on that list for someone else. Someone whose armor wouldn't tarnish.

Even if experience had taught her that such romantic fancies often led to trouble.

***

"Now that was a mighty tasty birthday feast." Henry wiped his mouth on the linen napkin and leaned back in his chair, nursing a final cup of tea.

"I second that." Christopher slathered his last mini scone with generous layers of wild strawberry jam and imported clotted cream. "Doesn't help the cholesterol, though."

"I'm eighty-five. If cholesterol hasn't gotten me yet, I doubt it will. And if it does"—he patted his midsection—"what a way to go."

"It's hard to argue with that."

Scanning the room, Henry folded his napkin and set it beside his plate. "I hope Marci remembers to stop by. She's a nice girl."

"Seems to be."

"She's not wearing a ring."

Uh-oh.

"She's also only here for a few weeks, Henry."

"Doesn't take long."

"For what?"

"To know if you click." A soft smile tugged at the older man's lips. "When I met Marjorie at that USO dance, we hit it off right away. I won't say it was love at first sight, but I knew the potential was there. We were married for fifty-four years, so I guess my instincts weren't too shabby."

Christopher wiped the residue of the jam off his fingers with the napkin. "Not everyone is blessed with sound instincts."

"You were. Otherwise you wouldn't be such a fine doctor."

"If that's true, my professional instincts didn't carry over to my personal life."

Henry leaned forward. "What happened with Denise wasn't your fault. The problem was her, not you. We've talked about this before."

Yeah, they had. One stormy night a few weeks into his stay,

after he'd pitched in to help his landlord batten down the gazebo his late wife had cherished.

But it had been a lost cause from the get-go. The brutal wind had ripped it apart, hurling pieces down the beach. Christopher had finally convinced the man to go inside, but he hadn't been able to pry Henry away from the window. And as tears streaked down his cheeks, he'd shared the story of how he'd built the gazebo for his beloved wife years ago. How it became her favorite place. And how it was the only spot where he could still feel her presence.

Christopher had stayed to console Henry. But later, over strong cups of coffee and a stubby candle to compensate for the electricity that had also been a victim of the storm, Henry had asked him about *his* life. And as the wind howled and the world was reduced to the diameter of a candle flame, he'd opened his heart—and sealed their friendship.

So Henry knew all about Denise.

But as much as Christopher had come to value the man's insights and advice on most topics, Denise was the exception.

"I'm not sure the problem was all hers, Henry. Besides, you didn't know her."

"I know you. That's enough."

Was it? When it came to blame, he—

"How was your tea, gentlemen?" Marci stopped beside their table, a small white box in hand.

"Best tea I ever went to," Henry declared.

Also the only one, as far as Christopher knew. "I didn't realize you were a tea aficionado."

Henry squinted at him. "If I knew what that word meant, I'd come up with a pithy reply. Why don't you give the lady *your* opinion."

"Very tasty. Thank you again for the invitation."

"It was the least I could do. I was in desperate straits the day you stopped by. The antibiotics worked magic." Transferring her attention to Henry, Marci set the small white box on the table. "Julie told me you were partial to the chocolate tarts, Mr. Calhoun. Here are a few more to take home so you can extend your birthday celebration."

"That's mighty sweet of you. And it's Henry, please. Now tell me, how are you enjoying Nantucket?"

"I'm afraid I haven't seen much yet. But I intend to make up for that as soon as my brother and sister-in-law get back."

"How long will you be staying?"

"I have five weeks left. One more to work, and four to play. I plan to take a month of vacation before I dive into a job search. I just finished my master's degree."

"In what?"

"Social work."

"My, that's impressive."

"Hardly." She gave a self-deprecating shrug. "Most people my age are already well-established in their careers. I was a late bloomer."

Henry cocked his head. "Not that late. You can't be more than twenty-four, twenty-five."

"Try thirty-one."

"Thirty-one. That's a perfect age."

At the sudden gleam in Henry's eyes, Christopher rejoined—and redirected—the conversation. "You're fortunate to have the chance to enjoy the island at leisure. Most visitors only stay for a weekend, or make it a day trip. You'll be able to explore all the beaches. And be sure to visit the lighthouses."

"Especially Sankaty." Henry jumped back in. "That's real close to where I live, in 'Sconset."

"I'll add that to my list."

"Tell you what. Why don't you ring me when you're out my way, and I'll ride along and give you the history. I could take you on a tour of the Lifesaving Museum too. I'm a trustee there. Then you could come back to my place and have a piece of my banana-nut bread. I don't make it as well as my wife did, but I like to keep it on hand. I think of her whenever I have a slice." His voice choked, and he fiddled with his napkin.

Marci's features softened. "I'd like that, Henry. And banana-nut bread is one of my favorites too."

"It's a date, then." He extracted a pen and small scrap of paper from his jacket, speaking as he wrote. "Here's my phone number. Give me a call anytime."

"I'll do that." Marci slipped the piece of paper into the pocket of her skirt.

"Maybe I can convince Christopher to join us, if he's not working. He's partial to my banana-nut bread too."

Marci took a small step back and clasped her hands in front of her. "I imagine Dr. Morgan is very busy, Henry. I'm on vacation. He's not."

"He works too hard. A little R & R would do him good. And you can call him Christopher. We don't stand on formality around here."

At her uncertain glance, Christopher spoke up. "Please do. Only my patients use my title—and we're beyond that."

She shifted her attention to him—and a faint, endearing flush suffused her cheeks.

It was Henry who finally broke the charged silence. "I think we're overstaying our welcome, Christopher." He swept a hand over the deserted tearoom, where Julie was beginning to clear tables. "These ladies have work to do."

Christopher pushed back his chair. "Sorry to hold you up."

"No problem." Marci touched his companion's arm. "I'll call you, Henry."

"That'll brighten up an old man's day."

In silence, Christopher followed him to the front door, taking his elbow as they descended the steps.

"She's a sweet girl." Henry kept a tight grip on the railing.

"Yes, she is."

"Great legs too."

Christopher reined in his grin. "You noticed?"

"Of course I noticed. My body may be old, but my heart's as young as it ever was. The question is, did you notice?"

"Yeah. I noticed."

"Hot dog! That's the best news I've heard in a month of Sundays."

Christopher called up his sternest tone. "Don't get any ideas, Henry."

"I wasn't the one with ideas back there." He waggled his eyebrows. "I saw the way you looked at her."

"She's an attractive woman. But appreciating beauty isn't the same as pursuing it."

"True—but it's a start."

Oh, brother.

Christopher opened the car door for his neighbor and expelled a breath.

Henry could be as tenacious as a Nantucket deer tick when he got a notion into his head. Trying to dissuade the older man from his fanciful conclusions would be difficult. The best he could do was avoid talking about Marci in Henry's presence.

Except he had a sneaking feeling Henry wasn't going to cooperate with that plan.

3

"I feel bad about putting you to this expense, JC."

Pushing through the half-moon gate in the tall privet hedge surrounding Edith's backyard, JC shot Marci a disgruntled look over his shoulder as she trailed along behind him. "We've been over this ad nauseam. After seven years of nonstop work and school, you deserve a vacation to celebrate your graduation. Since you won't stay with Heather and me, this is the best alternative."

"I can't stay with you. You're newlyweds. But this doesn't feel right, either." Marci followed her brother down a flagstone path through the well-tended yard. Considering the high prices on the island, her big brother was spending a fortune on the month's rent for the little outbuilding Chester had turned into a guest cottage.

JC stopped, set Marci's bags on a wooden bench, and took her shoulders in a firm grasp. "It's a gift, okay? All those years you worked long hours at the diner to support yourself while going to school, you wouldn't take a dime of help. None of the checks I sent you were ever cashed. I want to do this."

"I appreciate the gesture, JC—and I'm grateful." She folded her arms across her chest. "But I don't need my own cottage. The youth hostel would be fine. This is too expensive."

His intent gaze locked on hers. "You're worth every penny."

No, she wasn't. While her self-image *had* improved over the years, deep inside she still felt unworthy of such generosity and kindness.

When she didn't respond, JC scrutinized her, as if hoping to discover answers. "I've never understood why you have such a hard time valuing yourself."

And he never would, not if she had anything to say about it.

With his law-enforcement background, he could have discovered the truth long ago—but when she'd dropped out of school at nineteen and hit the road, promising to stay in touch if he gave her space, he'd kept his word.

He'd also kept his word five years later, when she'd told him she'd come home if he'd leave her past alone.

That's why she loved him—for his honor and integrity and unconditional love. He was the only person in her whole life she'd been able to count on, no matter what. The only person who had believed in her, who trusted in her basic goodness.

She could never jeopardize his opinion of her by telling him the truth.

It wasn't worth the risk.

Hugging herself tighter, she shrugged. "I just think you have better uses for your money."

He continued to study her for a few moments, then released her shoulders and picked up her bags again. "If it makes you feel less guilty, Edith gave me a discount. A bonus for my long tenure, as she put it. Most people only take island cottages for a week or two. I rented for a whole year—even during the quiet season, when she's normally closed. According to her, I was a bonanza." He gave an amused snort. "I've been called a lot of things in my life, but that was a new one."

As they approached the tiny clapboard cottage surrounded by budding hydrangea bushes, Marci stopped protesting. It wouldn't do any good anyway. JC was determined to give her a month of fun, and obsessing over the cost would ruin the gift for both of them.

Besides, he'd probably already paid the bill.

He set the bags by the door, turned the knob, and motioned her inside. "You're going to love this."

Easing past him, Marci stepped over the threshold. Froze. "Wow!"

Grinning, he nudged her farther in with his shoulder. "That's the reaction I was hoping for."

He edged around her as she took in the space she would call home for the next month. Though the structure was small, the vaulted ceiling and white walls gave it a feeling of spaciousness, and the blue-and-yellow color scheme created a cheery mood.

The compact unit was well-equipped too. A queen-size bed stood in the far corner, while closer to the door a small couch upholstered in hydrangea-print fabric and an old chest that served as a coffee table formed a sitting area. To the right of the front door a wooden café-sized table for two was tucked beside a window in a tiny kitchenette.

The place was like a display in a designer showroom.

In other words, it was a far cry from her tiny, decrepit apartment in Chicago, with its chipped avocado fixtures, burn-damaged Formica countertops, and stained linoleum. The same apartment she'd be returning to in a month, after this magical sojourn was over.

"Did you notice the pumpkin bread?"

JC's question distracted her from that depressing thought. "Where?"

He motioned toward a plastic-wrap-covered plate on the kitchen counter. "Edith left the same welcome gift for me. Trust me, there will be more. She'll take wonderful care of you."

Marci shoved her fingers into the pockets of her jeans. "I can take care of myself."

Huffing out a breath, JC pulled her into a bear hug. "What am I going to do with you?"

"Love me." The words came out muffled against his shirt as she hugged him back.

"Always." He gave her one more squeeze and stepped back. "Don't forget that Heather and I are taking you to dinner tomorrow." He held up his palm as she opened her mouth to protest. "No arguments. You've been outvoted." He clapped a hand over his mouth to cover a yawn. "Sorry. The jet lag is catching up with me."

"Go home. You guys must be dead on your feet after flying all day. I want to settle in anyway."

"Sounds like a plan. Want to join us for church tomorrow?"

She folded her arms and raised an eyebrow.

"Hey, you can't blame a guy for trying. We'll see you later in the day, then. Sleep well."

As he exited and shut the door, Marci once more gave her new digs an appreciative survey. Maybe all this would disappear in a month, as Cinderella's coach had vanished at the stroke of midnight—but in the meantime, she could pretend she was a princess. The only missing element was the handsome prince.

An image of Christopher Morgan flashed through her mind.

The tall, confident, charming doctor fit that description, no question about it.

But Hollywood-caliber looks and impeccable manners could be deceiving. A practiced rake could hide a callous, selfish heart until he got what he wanted—and princes could turn out to be scoundrels...leaving broken hearts, shattered dreams, and wrenching regrets in their wake.

Every instinct in her body said Christopher wasn't like that—but those same instincts had led her astray once.

And no way did she intend to trust them again.

* * *

Three days after the honeymooners returned—and two days into her vacation—Marci kept the promise she'd made to Henry two weeks before. After a morning spent soaking up rays on the beach, she'd driven to 'Sconset. True to his word, the older man had given her a tour of the area and invited her back to his home for refreshments.

"Your banana-nut bread is delicious, Henry."

He topped off Marci's coffee mug as they sat on his back porch. "Glad you liked it."

"The tour was fabulous too. I can't believe they actually moved Sankaty Light."

"Yep. It was quite a feat. Made the national news, even. Cost a bundle of money, but that was the only way to save it from tumbling into the sea, what with all the erosion over there. Moved it inch by inch. Slow and steady."

"Slow and steady is always a sound plan. With lighthouses—and life." Marci took a sip of her coffee as she gazed at the sea, separated from Henry's backyard by only a picket fence and a stretch of beach.

"I expect that's true, in general. I know my Marjorie felt like that about her garden. She had the patience of Job with all these plants." He waved a hand over the curving, overgrown flower beds that hugged much of the picket fence and porch, leaving only a small bit of lush green grass in the center and back of the yard. "She tucked them into the ground, nurtured them, did all she could to help them flourish. Started most everything from seeds and cuttings. I often told her it would be faster to buy established plants, but she claimed flowers grew better if they had a stable home from the beginning."

A sudden film of moisture clouded Marci's vision. "Your wife was a wise woman." Under Henry's intent scrutiny, she shifted in her seat and stabbed another bite of banana-nut bread. As she'd already learned, the older man was an astute observer—and fending off questions wasn't in her plans for this visit. "Did she spend a lot of time in her garden?"

"Practically lived out here in the summer—not that you'd know it now." He inspected the weed-choked beds and sighed. "I tried to keep up with the garden for the first few years after she died, but arthritis finally did me in. Bending isn't as easy as it used to be. Makes me sad, how much they've deteriorated."

"How long has your wife been gone?"

"An eternity." He drew in a slow breath. Let it out. "Feels that long anyway, after more than half a century of marriage. But to be exact, ten years and two months."

It was nice to know some relationships lasted.

Marci studied the garden in which Marjorie Calhoun had invested so much labor and love. Despite the neglect, hints of its former beauty remained. Here and there, hardy flowers poked through the rampant weeds. Although out-of-control ivy was attempting to choke a circle of hydrangeas in one corner, the bushes were sporting buds. And a climbing rose in desperate need of pruning competed for fence space with a tangle of morning-glory vines behind a large birdbath.

"What was over there, Henry?" Marci indicated the hydrangeas, which rimmed a spot bare except for some low-growing foliage that could be weeds.

"Used to be a gazebo. I built it for Marjorie years ago. She loved to sit out there with a glass of lemonade after she worked in the garden and enjoy the fruits of her labors. Lost it in a storm winter before last."

Marci rubbed a finger over the peeling white paint on the arm of her wicker rocker, mulling over all Henry had told her during their sightseeing outing. About Nantucket—and his life.

He hadn't dwelt on his tribulations, focusing instead on the positive experiences that had graced his eighty-five years. Yet there had been problems, referenced only in passing. Henry had watched friends die in battle. Nursed his wife through a cancer scare. And now he struggled to maintain the life he loved as his vigor and strength ebbed and the cost of living on the island soared.

It seemed long life was both a blessing and a curse.

As if he'd read her mind, Henry angled toward her, the afternoon sunlight highlighting the crevices on his face. "I'll tell you a secret, Marci. Growing old isn't for sissies."

Pressure built in her throat, and she leaned over to place a hand on his gnarled fingers. "Your body may be old, but your spirit is young. And I suspect it always will be."

He patted her hand. "Thank you, my dear."

As she finished her sweet treat and gave the garden another sweep, an idea began to take shape in her mind. "Can you distinguish between the weeds and flowers, Henry?"

"Yes."

"Then why don't we clean this place up? You can point out the weeds until I learn which is which, and I can pull them up."

"I didn't invite you here today to work."

She dismissed his comment with a flip of her hand. "I've worked my whole life. I can't lie around on a beach every day for the next month. I'll go stir-crazy. I need to do something productive too. This would be a challenge. And it would be fun. I bet we could whip this place into shape in a matter of days."

"You may not think it's fun after you get blisters on your hands. Besides, gardening is hard work. It takes strength and stamina. Lifting, digging, pulling. You're kind of a little thing."

"Think of me as small but mighty. I've spent half my life juggling heavy trays of dishes and glasses. I've moved tables, hauled and stacked chairs, and run up and down stairs balancing plates of food. At Ronnie's Diner, I'm known as the Bionic Blonde. Trust me, being a waitress is a tough job. I'm a whole lot stronger than I look."

He considered her, a spark of enthusiasm igniting in his faded blue irises. "Well, I sure would like to see this place the way it used to be. And I know Marjorie would be pleased."

"Then it's decided. Heather and JC said I could use their car every afternoon, so I can bike to a beach and play in the sand in the morning, then come out here and play in the dirt after lunch. What do you say?"

A slow grin creased his face. "I say let's do it."

* * *

Christopher wheeled his bike behind his cottage, glanced toward Henry's backyard—and came to an abrupt halt.

What was Marci Clay doing on her hands and knees between two hydrangea bushes in Henry's garden?

As she began to tug on an object out of his line of sight, Henry's voice rang across the yards. "Hey, Christopher! Come see what we're doing!"

Marci lost her grip, flailed, and plopped back on her bottom.

"Hi, Henry. Hello, Marci."

Instead of responding to his greeting, she scrambled to her feet and wiped her palms on her jeans.

"We're cleaning out the garden." Henry aimed his shovel toward a large pile of wilting weeds and ivy.

Christopher set his mail on the railing of his tiny back porch and strolled over to the picket fence that separated the yards. In the far corner of Henry's garden, plants had emerged from the jumble of weeds. Gardening had never been one of his interests, but his mother had enjoyed the hobby and he'd learned a few basics from her. Enough to recognize the unearthed peony buds and coral bells. The other plants Marci had rescued were a mystery.

"You've made an impressive start." He turned his attention to Marci, who hovered in the distance. Her jeans were grimy, her fingernails caked with mud. Sweat had wiped her face clean of makeup. One of her cheeks sported a long streak of dirt.

None of that detracted from her appeal.

Ignoring the sudden uptick in his pulse, Christopher tried for a casual smile. "I see Henry put you to work."

"I volunteered."

"She's a hard worker too." Henry rested the shovel against the fence. "Why are you home so early?"

"It's almost six-thirty."

"Six-thirty!" Shock rippled across Marci's face. "Henry, I've got to go. I told Edith and Chester I'd have dinner with them tonight. At seven." She rubbed her hands on her jeans again and dashed for the porch. "But I'll be back tomorrow."

"Are you still sure you want to do this?"

"Yes." She snatched up her purse and rummaged through it.

"I never leave a job unfinished."

Henry shot him a pointed look. "Maybe you could walk Marci to her car."

"Oh, no, that's all right, Henry." Marci pulled out her keys, and his gaze dropped to a long scratch on the back of her hand. "I'm right in front. He doesn't need to bother." Before either of them could respond, she jogged toward the gate. "See you tomorrow, Henry."

Christopher frowned after her. What was it about him that made her act like one of the island deer that bolted when anyone got too close?

And why did he care? Hadn't he gone out of his way for more than two years to discourage any woman who tried to cozy up to him? He should be grateful for her lack of interest.

Except he wasn't—Lord help him.

An engine started, followed by the crunch of car tires on the oystershell lane. Slowly the sound receded as she drove away.

Turning his attention back to Henry, he swept a hand over the garden. "How did all this start?"

His neighbor scratched his head. "Beats me. One minute we were talking about Marjorie, and the next thing I knew Marci was pulling weeds. She's strong too, just like she told me. Claims it comes from all those years of waitressing."

"Marci was a waitress?"

"Yep. That's how she put herself through school. You've got to admire her spunk."

At the very least.

"What else did she tell you?" Christopher tried for nonchalance.

"Mostly we talked about flowers. But I expect we'll get into a lot of other subjects as we work on the garden. Maybe you could stop by one afternoon and join us for lemonade."

Bad idea. Contact could lead to connection, and he wasn't in the market for a romantic relationship—even if the woman was willing. And Marci obviously wasn't.

Besides, she had issues—as evidenced by her tears the first night in the restaurant, her skittishness, and her wary attitude.

That could be dangerous.

"She makes you nervous, doesn't she?"

Wonderful.

Now he had an armchair psychologist analyzing him in his backyard.

Ignoring Henry's remark, Christopher scanned the sky as a gust of wind whipped past. "I think a storm may be brewing."

His neighbor stacked his hands on top of the handle of the shovel, watching him. "Yep. I'd say there could be unsettled weather ahead."

He was out of here.

"I'm going to rescue my mail." Christopher backed toward his porch.

"Taking cover, hmm? Good luck." Smirking, Henry ambled back to his hydrangeas.

The older man's meaning was clear. Henry thought he was running scared.

Truth be told, he was. If taking cover was the coward's way out, so be it. At least he'd be safe.

And if Henry and Edith were hoping to match him up with the attractive blonde, they were going to be disappointed.

Because he wasn't ready to get serious about anyone.

Especially a woman whose eyes held secrets.

4

Marci gave the clouds massing on the horizon a wary inspection as she drove down Milestone Road toward Henry's house on Wednesday. They'd begun to gather while she'd lounged on the beach this morning, and they'd grown more ominous during her brief stop at her cottage to eat lunch and change into work clothes. If they continued to build, her gardening efforts would be curtailed this afternoon.

For now, though, the sun was shining on the windswept moors and cranberry bog to her left. Already this long stretch of undulating road had become one of her favorite spots. Far less populated than other parts of the island, the pristine beauty and serenity of the simple, timeless landscape was calming.

And she needed calming—thanks to a certain heartthrob-handsome doctor with eyes the color of a Nantucket sky.

She tapped a finger against the wheel and blew out a breath.

How had he managed to get under her skin—and disrupt her equilibrium—after a few short encounters?

It didn't make sense.

And trying to figure it out was giving her a headache.

Enough about Christopher Morgan. While keeping him out of her dreams was beyond her control, she didn't have to think about him while she was awake.

Redirecting her attention to the bike path that followed the road toward 'Sconset, she focused on the cyclists. They were out in force today. Family groups for the most part, with a few couples here and there.

The solitary biker up ahead, on the outskirts of the village, was an anomaly. A man in jeans, the wire baskets on the back of his bike loaded down. With what? Paraphernalia for a beach outing? Picnic food? Curious that he was alone.

As Marci passed the bike, she gave him a quick glance.

Her jaw dropped.

It was Christopher Morgan.

Reflexes kicking in, she pressed on the accelerator. Not until she was well past him did she risk a peek in her rearview mirror.

What in the world was he doing on a bicycle? Didn't doctors usually drive luxury cars? And why wasn't he working on a weekday?

With those questions tumbling through her mind, Marci navigated the narrow streets of the tiny village, pulled to a stop in front of Henry's cottage—and remained there, engine idling.

Now what?

She'd planned to be gone long before Christopher arrived home. Now, the only way to avoid another unsettling encounter would be to put the car back in gear, drive away, and call Henry with her regrets.

While she hated to disappoint the older man, that seemed the safest course.

Before she could follow through with her plan, however, Henry's front door opened. He pushed through, strolled over to the car, and leaned down to peer in the open passenger-side window. "Thought I heard a car stop. Kept waiting for you to knock. Everything okay?"

She was stuck.

"Yes." Marci shut off the engine, picked up her purse, and opened her door as Christopher rounded the corner on his bike.

"Hey, Christopher!" Henry straightened up and waved.

Christopher raised one hand in response.

"What's he doing on a bike?" Marci stayed behind Henry.

"Always rides it to work in pleasant weather. Sometimes in not-so-pleasant weather. Says it helps keep him in shape."

No question about it. There wasn't an ounce of fat on his toned, fit form as he pedaled toward them.

"What's he doing home on a weekday?"

"He only has office hours until noon on Wednesdays. Then he works three to eleven in the ER. Spends too many hours on the job, if you ask me. The man needs a few diversions."

At the speculative glint in his eyes, Marci smothered a sigh. Henry seemed tuned to the same channel as Edith.

All the more reason to keep her distance. The sparks already flying didn't need any encouragement.

Christopher glided to a stop beside them and straddled the bike. "Hi."

The way her heart melted at his smile you'd think she was an innocent, starry-eyed teen in the throes of her first crush. And she was none of the above.

"Hi." Her reply sounded stiff. Bordering on unfriendly.

Henry squinted at her before turning his attention to Christopher. "Was the prescription ready?"

"Yes." Christopher pulled two grocery bags out of one of the wire baskets and handed them to the older man. "I think I got everything else on your list too. I also threw in a couple of sugar doughnuts from The Flake."

"You didn't have to do that." Henry took the bags. "But I'm glad you did."

"I thought you might be." Christopher grinned and swung his leg over the bar on the bike. "There's a pair of garden gloves in there too—for your new assistant. Gardening is hard on the hands." He turned to her. "How's the scratch?"

Was there anything this man *didn't* notice?

Marci shoved her right hand deeper into her pocket to hide the souvenir of her tussle with a rose bush the first day. "It's fine. I'll be happy to reimburse you for the gloves."

"No way." Henry shook his head. "If anyone's going to repay him, it's me. The cost of a pair of garden gloves is a small price to pay for all the free labor I'm getting. Add it to my tab."

"It's no big deal." Christopher took off his helmet. "I have to grab a quick bite before I go to the hospital. See you later."

Without waiting for a response, he pushed his bike around the corner of his cottage.

"He's a fine young man. Been almost like a son to me these past two years." Henry started toward the gate to the backyard.

"Let me take a bag." Marci tugged one of the plastic sacks out of his hand. "Have you only known him for two years?"

"Yep. That's when he moved to the island from Boston. Marjorie and I used to rent out the cottage to summer people, but when Christopher offered to sign a one-year lease, I grabbed it. It's less hassle than having new people come and go every week, and now I have income for the whole year, not just for the summer. He renewed again last month. Can't imagine not having him around anymore—but I expect one of these days he'll go home."

Raising the question of why he'd come to Nantucket in the first place.

Marci had to bite it back as they reached the porch. "Would you like me to bring this inside for you or hand it through the door?"

"Come on in." He pulled open the screen door and stepped aside to let her pass. "Don't mind the dust. I'm not much of a housekeeper."

Marci walked through the small mudroom and set the bag on the Formica counter in the kitchen. Though the room was dated, yellow curtains added a bright spot of color, and the pine table for four tucked into a windowed alcove offered a view into the backyard and the sea beyond. There *was* a bit of dust on the lower cabinets, but the countertops were clutter-free and the sink had been wiped clean. A dishrag was draped over the chrome faucet, and a neatly folded towel had been tucked into the handle of the oven.

"That's my Marjorie." He pointed to a framed photo on the wall near the table. "I put that picture there so I can see her while I eat. I never did like to eat alone."

She crossed the room to examine it.

The photo had been taken in Henry's backyard and featured the gazebo, the structure's weathered patina the color of driftwood. A slim older woman, a basket of cut flowers in hand, stood at the entrance below a band of lattice.

"She was lovely, Henry."

"Inside and out. My daughter resembles her."

Marci shifted toward him. "Does she live on the island?"

His expression grew melancholy. "No. Boston. She doesn't get down this way very often."

"Any other children?"

"No. Not that we wouldn't have welcomed a houseful, but the good Lord just gave us one." He motioned toward the door. "Shall we get to work? With the clouds rolling in, I expect this will be a short day."

"I'm all set."

"Let me put away the perishables and find those gloves Christopher bought. Mighty thoughtful of him. But that's the kind of man he is." He rummaged through the bag as he spoke. "Last winter I had a nasty bout of pneumonia. Was weak as a kitten for weeks. Christopher came over to see me twice a day and brought me food every night. Watched old movies with me too, even though he meets himself coming and going." He withdrew the gloves and handed them over.

Marci fingered the soft leather. No cheap cloth gloves for Christopher Morgan. These were high-quality. Expensive.

In other words, too nice for her.

JC would have a fit if he was privy to that sort of thinking—but despite the strides she'd made with self-esteem, it was hard to quash the feeling that she didn't deserve such generosity.

For once, however, she didn't mistrust the motive. Christopher had never suggested she was in his debt for the house call. Nor was he likely to expect anything in return for this considerate gesture. His motives weren't suspect, unlike those of previous male gift-givers.

He seemed, as Henry had indicated, to simply be a good man.

The kind of man she'd always dreamed of finding.

But the chances of those dreams coming true were negligible.

Because no matter how much her self-image improved, it would have to take a quantum leap for her to feel worthy of someone like Christopher Morgan.

* * *

"So, what have you been doing to amuse yourself on your much-deserved vacation?" JC passed a bowl of mashed potatoes to Marci.

She took it and scooped a generous portion onto her plate,

then handed it to Heather. All the gardening must be giving her appetite a boost. "Do you know Henry Calhoun?"

Heather propped her elbows on the small oak table in the corner of The Devon Rose kitchen. "Isn't he the older gentleman in 'Sconset, JC? The one the church youth group did some painting for last summer when my nephew was here?"

"Yeah. That's Henry. How do you know him, Marci?"

"He came to tea while you were gone and we hit it off." She filled them in on the background. "So I spend my mornings on the beach and my afternoons at Henry's playing in the dirt. He's a great guy. Eighty-five years old. Taught English at the high school until he retired, and he still tutors. He's a trustee at the Lifesaving Museum too."

"Wait a minute. Back up. You're doing yard work?" JC furrowed his brow. "This is supposed to be a vacation."

"Trust me, this *is* a vacation. I don't have to get up at the crack of dawn to sling hash at Ronnie's. I don't have to stay up until two in the morning working on term papers or studying for tests. I'm living in a cottage that belongs in the pages of *House Beautiful*. I have no schedule to keep, and I'm loving every minute of it. But the truth is, I'm used to being busy. If all I did was sit around on the beach day after day, I'd go nuts."

JC took a sip of water. "Is that how you got the scratch on your hand? Gardening?"

She examined the long, jagged abrasion. "Sometimes to uncover beauty you have to deal with a few thorns. But this won't happen again. I have garden gloves now."

"Did you get them at Bartlett's Farm?" Heather asked. "They have a great garden center."

Marci dug into her mashed potatoes. "No. Um...Henry's neighbor got me a pair. Did you put an unusual seasoning in these? They're delicious."

"A touch of garlic salt."

"Are you talking about the ER doc who lives next door? Why would he get you gloves?" JC stopped eating.

"What difference does it make?"

He set his fork down. "Why are you evading the question?"

"I'm not evading the question. But why are you playing detective? You're supposed to be off-duty now."

Heather looked back and forth between the two of them. "JC, why don't you show your sister the drawing from Nathan? You'll love it, Marci. We sent him a photo of The Devon Rose, and he did an incredible pen-and-ink sketch of it as a wedding present. It was in that package that arrived while we were on our honeymoon. I'm going to frame it and hang it in the foyer." When her new husband didn't respond, Heather nudged him. "JC?"

"Yeah." After a few beats he rose, retrieved the sketch, and held it out without a word.

Marci set aside her fork and took it. The detailed rendering was not only technically accurate, but also managed to imbue The Devon Rose with a sort of magical ambiance. "Wow. Who knew he had this kind of talent all these years?"

"It's hard to shine if you're serving time for armed robbery. But I think he has a bright future ahead now that he's started down a new path."

"According to his last letter, it sounds like he's on track to finish his GED by the end of the summer." Marci handed the drawing back to JC.

"That's the plan. He just needs to hang in for one more year."

"He wouldn't have such a hopeful future without you—and all those letters you sent him through the years that you thought he ignored."

A flush crept across her brother's cheeks as he set the

drawing aside. "God can take most of the credit for his turnaround."

Heather entwined her fingers with her husband's. "But you did play a major role. You've been a wonderful brother to both your siblings."

"I second that." Marci lifted her water glass in tribute. JC's love for her and Nathan had never wavered, despite the trouble and heartaches they'd given him.

He was one in a million.

But the more she saw of—and heard about—a certain 'Sconset doctor, the more she was beginning to believe he might qualify for membership in that exclusive club.

5

Why wasn't Henry answering her knock?

Marci tapped her garden gloves against her palm. Usually he met her at the front door—but she *was* a few minutes late.

Maybe he was waiting for her in the yard.

She circled the house, pausing to inhale the heady, old-fashioned scent of the pink roses clinging to the arbor that arched over the gate to the side yard. Given the profusion of buds she'd uncovered after untwining the ivy and wild morning-glory vines from the hardy canes—and incurring that nasty scratch in the process—the bush would be a showstopper in another couple of weeks.

"Henry, are you back here?" Marci pushed through the gate, clicking it shut behind her.

No response.

Strange.

If he wasn't in the house or the yard, where was he?

A few seconds later, when she rounded the corner of the clapboard cottage and stepped into the backyard, she got her answer.

The older man was lying on the ground, the bowl of the concrete birdbath upside down on his chest—and he wasn't moving.

She froze for an instant, heart slamming against her rib cage. Then she raced across the lawn and dropped down beside him. Reached for his hand. It was cold.

"Henry? Henry, can you hear me?"

At her frantic question, his eyelids fluttered open. For a moment he seemed disoriented. Then he blinked and squinted at her. "Hey, Marci. Got myself...into a real pickle...didn't I?" The gasped words were etched with pain.

But at least he was conscious. That had to be a positive sign.

"Don't move, Henry."

"Can't. That's why...I'm here."

Stay calm, Marci. Think this through.

Trying to heed that advice, she took a quick inventory.

The bowl of the birdbath was resting on the ground on Henry's left side. That would give her leverage to push it off without putting any more pressure on his chest.

She moved to his right side, knelt, and grasped the elevated edge of the bowl. "I'm going to lift this off of you, Henry. Hang on."

Taking a deep breath, she tightened her grip—and inch by inch, muscles straining, she raised the heavy, oversized concrete basin.

When it was standing on end on Henry's left side, she rose and stepped over him, keeping a firm grip on the concrete edge. Then she lowered the bowl to the ground.

"That's a relief. Thank you."

Henry started to move, but Marci pressed him back with a hand on his shoulder as she knelt beside him. He was far too pale, and his skin still felt cold—and clammy. "Does anything hurt?"

"My left side is kind of sore. Might have cracked a rib." He peered up at her. "You're a mite fuzzy too."

"I'm calling 911." She fumbled in her purse for her cell. Latched onto it. But her fingers were shaking so badly it took two tries to punch in the emergency number. As she waited for the call to go through, she rested one hand on Henry's shoulder and did her best to sound calm. "Just stay still, Henry. Help will be here soon."

While answering the dispatcher's questions, Marci kept watch over the older man. His eyelids had drifted closed again, and she took his hand, pressing her thumb to his wrist.

"Ticker's still working, if that's what you're checking."

At his wry comment, her lips twitched despite the gravity of the situation. "The ambulance is on the way." She shoved the phone back into her purse.

"Last ambulance that came here was for Marjorie, when she had her heart attack. She never came home."

Marci's throat tightened. "This isn't a heart attack. You'll be back. We're not finished with the garden yet."

He gave her hand a squeeze. "You're a good girl, Marci." His voice was weakening.

Another wave of panic swept over her. "How long ago did you fall, Henry?"

"I came out about noon. Thought I'd move the birdbath, since we were going to work in that section today. Guess I'm not as strong as I thought I was. Used to be able to lift stuff like that with no problem. But I twisted my ankle when I turned, and I lost my balance. Fell back with the bowl on top of me. Not my most graceful moment."

She scanned her watch. He'd been lying out here fifteen minutes before she arrived.

Too long if there was any internal damage.

The faint wail of a siren pierced the air. The seven-mile trip from the main town wouldn't take long—but every minute felt like an eternity.

"Sorry for all this trouble, Marci."

"Don't worry about it, Henry. Accidents happen. I just want you to get back on your feet fast so we can finish this garden before I leave."

His grip loosened. "Might not happen, Marci."

Her stomach bottomed out. "Of course it will."

The corners of his mouth rose a hair. "I like your spirit. You'd be good for Christopher, you know. That boy needs a woman like you." He was starting to drift.

She didn't respond—and he didn't press his point.

But he was wrong. Christopher did *not* need a woman like her—for reasons she'd never tell Henry. Why tarnish her relationship with the older man by sharing her sordid history?

Flashing lights appeared in the distance as the wailing ambulance came down the tiny byway in front of the cottage, but she didn't relinquish her grip on Henry's hand until the EMTs pushed through the back gate and joined her.

They went to work at once, tossing her questions while they started an IV and took Henry's vitals. Most of the terminology they bantered back and forth was Greek to her, but she gleaned enough to determine his blood pressure was low and that they were concerned about the pain on his left side.

When they were ready to transport, Henry turned her way. "Would you call Christopher?"

"Yes—and I'll follow you to the hospital too."

He lifted a hand in acknowledgment, then closed his eyes.

After the technicians loaded him into the ambulance, Marci slid into her car and fell in behind the vehicle as it pulled away from Henry's cottage.

Once she was on Milestone Road accelerating for the main town, she googled Christopher's number and tapped it in.

"Family Medical. How may I help you?"

"I'm trying to reach Dr. Morgan. Is he in?"

"Yes. He's with a patient. May I have him return your call later this afternoon?"

Not ideal—but all she could do was leave a detailed message, along with her cell number.

The woman promised to catch him between patients.

When her cell rang less than five minutes later, she snatched it off the seat beside her. "Christopher?"

"Yes. What happened?" Worry underscored his clipped question.

She filled him in. "Do you think he could have broken a rib or two?"

"It's possible. I'll call the ER and let them know I want to be kept informed. Where are you?"

"Following the ambulance."

"I'll get to the hospital as soon as I can, but I've got a full patient load this afternoon. I'll call you if I hear any news."

"Thanks."

"How are *you* doing?"

She blinked at the quiet, caring question. "I'm not the one who fell."

"Accidents are traumatic for everyone."

At the warmth in his voice, her vision misted. "It was scary—and I didn't like feeling h-helpless." Crud. She clamped her lips together. Getting emotional was *not* in keeping with the strong, independent image she cultivated. Tightening her grip on the wheel, she hardened her voice. "But, hey, I'm a tough chick. You don't have to worry about me."

A few beats passed—and when Christopher responded, his gentle tone suggested her bravado hadn't fooled him. "Hang in there. We'll get him through this. I'll be in touch." The line went dead.

Marci dropped the phone into her lap.

We'll get through this.

That had a nice ring to it. Like they'd work together to cope with whatever lay ahead. As partners. Henry would benefit from that. The more people in his corner, the better.

But wouldn't it be wonderful if their partnership could extend beyond this emergency?

Marci snorted.

Like that would happen.

Much as she wished she could change the past, it would shape her future forever.

And because of it, her chances of finding a man like Christopher to be her partner for life had vanished as completely as Henry's beloved gazebo.

* * *

Christopher swung into the hospital parking lot and propped his bike against the back wall of the ER. Leaving in the middle of office hours would put him way behind and aggravate waiting patients—but the news he'd received ten minutes ago had warranted a quick trip to the hospital.

Pushing through the staff entrance, he spotted the senior doctor on duty getting ready to enter an examining room. "Jack!" The fiftyish man with salt-and-pepper hair turned at the summons, waiting as Christopher hurried toward him. "Where's Henry?"

"Room three. He's being prepped."

"I'll make a quick stop there first. I also want to take a look at the CT scan. Is David here?" Thank goodness they had a topnotch surgeon on staff.

"He's en route."

"Thanks." Christopher peeled off and strode toward room three. Two nurses were with Henry, but they edged aside to allow him to move in close.

The view knotted his stomach. Other than the bout with pneumonia, the man who'd become like a second grandfather had always been healthy.

But he didn't look healthy now. His color was bad, and deep crevices lined his face. Under the sheet, his thin frame seemed barely there.

Henry's eyelids fluttered open. "Hey, Christopher."

"Hello, Henry. I hear you had a fall."

"Yep. They gave me the bad news."

"You on board with the plan?"

"Do I have a choice?"

"Yes—but this is what I'd recommend."

"The other doc told me the same thing. So I said go ahead." He reached out a hand, and Christopher took his gnarled fingers. "Thanks for coming. Sorry for the bother."

His throat constricted. "It's no bother, Henry. Marci's here too."

"I know. They told me. Go find her and tell her to go home. No point hanging around a hospital unless you get hauled here like I did."

"I'll see what I can do. I also called your daughter."

Henry grimaced. "I bet she threw a hissy fit."

"Not quite." But close. Her rant about stubborn old men who refused to listen to reason had singed his ear. "She's coming down tomorrow."

Henry sighed. "Better batten down the hatches." He pulled his hand free and waved toward the door. "Go see that little lady in the waiting room. And tell her not to worry about me. If it's my time, it's my time. I'm ready. Besides, there's no sense fretting over spilled milk—or foolish old men."

"It isn't your time. Not if we have anything to say about it. And we'll talk about the foolish part later." He took Henry's hand again and gave it an encouraging squeeze. "God be with you, my friend."

He exited the examining room, commandeered one of the ER computers, and pulled up Henry's CT scan.

As he studied it, the senior doctor joined him. "What do you think?"

"Same as you. Grade two, borderline three." Christopher pointed to the abdominal cavity. "We may need to transfuse."

"Agreed. We're keeping a close watch on blood count and pressure."

With a nod, Christopher stood. "A friend of Henry's is in the waiting room. I'll brief her before I go back to the office. Will you call me with any updates?"

"You got it." The man moved on to his patient.

Christopher strode through the ER intake area and stepped into the large waiting room. A number of people were lounging in the chairs, reading magazines or newspapers. Everyone looked up when he entered—but Marci wasn't among them.

Only after he moved farther into the irregularly shaped room did he spot her.

She was staring out a window in the far corner, arms crossed tight over her chest, posture rigid, her distress almost palpable. Hard as she tried to present a tough front to the world, she had a tender, caring heart beneath that veneer—as this unguarded moment confirmed.

As he closed the distance between them, she turned.

Blanched. Shot to her feet. "What are you doing here? Is Henry..." Her voice choked.

"No." He took her arm and eased her into a chair, fighting off the urge to pull her into a comforting hug. "I came over between patients."

"Why?" She searched his face. "It's more than a cracked rib, isn't it?"

"Yes. His ribs are fine. But he has a lacerated spleen and internal bleeding."

She sucked in a breath. "I had a feeling it was bad. What happens now?"

"If Henry was younger, we'd take a conservative approach and let the spleen try to heal on its own—but that treatment option hasn't been very successful in patients over fifty-five. So we're going to remove it."

"What's the downside of that?"

"Short-term, the typical risks of any surgery. Long-term, greater susceptibility to infections."

Marci linked her fingers into a tight knot in her lap. "How long will the surgery take?"

"Two or three hours. Henry said I should tell you to go home."

"Forget it."

"I had a feeling you'd say that."

"How long will he be in here?"

"If all goes well, four or five days."

"Then what?"

That was a harder question to answer.

"I'm not sure. Recovery can take months—and he'll need a fair amount of help initially."

She bit her lower lip. "While we were waiting for the

ambulance, he told me his wife never came home after she was taken to the hospital. I got the feeling he thinks that will be true for him too."

"Same here—but I'm going to do everything I can to make certain that doesn't happen. He's very active and healthy for his age. Other than arthritis, not much slows him down. There's no reason he can't recover from this—unless he gives up."

"He's not the type to do that."

"That could change if his independence is compromised—or if he has to leave his cottage. I've seen it happen."

Marci studied him, her features softening. "You're not talking about your experience with patients, are you?"

Man, this woman had excellent instincts. And a well of compassion—and empathy—that ran deep. She was going to excel at social work.

"No. I saw it happen with my grandfather." Tempted as he was to tell her more, there was no time for a prolonged discussion. "I have a waiting room full of patients, but I'll be back as soon as I can. In the meantime, I'll stay in touch with the hospital and let you know if I hear any news. But you may want to run home for a while. Henry's right. There's nothing you can do here while he's in surgery."

She wiggled her foot and stared at the toe of her sports shoe. "Leaving doesn't feel right. It would be sad to be in surgery and think no one cared enough to hang around." She lifted her chin. "Would you tell him I'm staying?"

Why was he not surprised?

"Yes. I'll run back and talk to him before I leave."

"Thanks." She slumped against the wall and refolded her arms across her chest. Seeming once again in need of a reassuring hug.

But he quashed that impulse.

Because Marci had done nothing to encourage that kind of gesture—and he couldn't offer reassurances when he had no idea what the future held for Henry.

6

After a third rumble from her stomach, Marci rose and began pacing. Maybe moving would quiet its complaints. Or mask the noise, if nothing else.

In the three hours since Christopher had left her in the waiting room, the cast of characters around her had turned over at least twice. And still no word about Henry.

Had everyone forgotten she was here—including Christopher?

Could she throw herself on the mercy of the woman at the ER intake desk, see what information she could glean?

Why not? She had nothing to lose.

She struck off for the door—just as Christopher pushed through.

Her pulse leapt, and she met him halfway as he wove toward her. "Well?"

"He's out of surgery. Everything went well, and he didn't need a transfusion. He'll be in recovery for a while, then moved to a regular room later tonight."

The tension in her shoulders eased. "Can I see him?"

"Not yet. He won't be coherent for an hour or two."

Her stomach rumbled again, and heat suffused her cheeks. "Sorry. Must be the stress."

"Or hunger. Did you eat lunch?"

"I had a container of yogurt. I wasn't hungry."

"Sounds like you are now. Why don't we go get a quick bite? After that, you should be able to see him for a few minutes."

Before she could process the unexpected invitation, her phone began to vibrate.

Saved by the bell.

"Excuse me for a second." She pulled the cell from her pocket. Scanned the screen before putting it to her ear. "Hi, JC."

"Marci? Are you okay? We got worried when you didn't return the car."

"Yeah, I'm fine. Henry had an accident, and I've been at the ER all afternoon."

"What happened?"

She gave him a quick rundown. "If you don't need the car tonight, I'd like to hang around a while."

"No. We're planning a quiet evening at home. You want us to bring dinner over for you?"

She glanced at Christopher, who'd moved a discreet distance away. The wise course would be to accept JC's offer. But a break from the hospital would be welcome—and what harm could there be in having a casual meal with Henry's neighbor? "I, uh, already have other plans."

"With who? I didn't think you knew anyone here other than me and Heather and Edith and Chester. Have you met...wait." A beat ticked by. "You do know Henry's neighbor—aka 'the glove man.' Is he taking you to dinner?"

With his superb deductive reasoning, it was no wonder her brother was such an outstanding detective. "No comment."

"That tells me all I need to know. And for the record, from what I've seen of Christopher Morgan, he's one of the good guys.

It's about time you went out on a date."

"It's not a..." She angled away from Christopher and lowered her voice. "Goodbye, JC." She punched the end button with more force than necessary.

"Your brother?" Christopher rejoined her.

"Yes." She dropped the phone into her purse. "How did you know?"

"I recognize the initials. We attend the same church, and I run into him on occasion in the ER when he's on duty. Seems like a nice guy."

"He is. Also nosy."

Christopher flashed her a smile. "I know what it's like to have a hovering big brother—and I expect it's worse for a younger sister. So can I interest you in food? Downyflake is only a five-minute walk in case anything comes up with Henry."

The family vibe at the local hangout, with its bright lights that neutralized any romantic ambiance, was ideal—and she was starving.

"I'm in."

"Great. Watch your step, though. They're replacing a few of the slabs in the sidewalk."

He took her arm as they exited the ER—an impersonal, polite gesture indicative of breeding and polished manners, nothing more.

Yet as they strolled down the sidewalk, his protective hand guiding her around the rough patches, what was the harm in pretending for just a few minutes that his touch meant far more?

* * *

Fifteen minutes later, seated on opposite sides of a booth, Christopher dived into his hearty bowl of quahog chowder.

Marci wasn't far behind.

"This is amazing." She added a few more oyster crackers to her bowl and stirred them in.

"It's hard to go wrong with the local specialty."

"I've only had it once since I've been here."

"The night I saw you in the restaurant."

Her spoon froze for an instant, midway between bowl and mouth—and heat crept up his neck.

Bad blunder.

"Sorry. I shouldn't have brought that up. But it's been on my mind. You seemed...rattled...that night."

She went back to eating. "That was the day of the wedding. I was a little emotional." She chased a quahog around the soup. "To be honest, I'm surprised you noticed what I was eating. I got the distinct impression your attention was elsewhere." Her tone was light. The echo of pain in her eyes wasn't.

"Guilty as charged—a lapse for which I've already apologized."

"I appreciate that. Unfortunately, my physical assets are often all people notice."

He stirred his chowder. "I noticed more than that."

"Right. My soup."

"No. I also noticed you were crying. In all honesty, that's what I noticed *first*."

She stirred her chowder, chin down. "I don't usually cry in public. Watching JC get married...it kind of choked me up." She scooped up a spoonful of chowder. "Tell me about the grandfather you mentioned earlier."

There was more to the restaurant story than she was telling—

but she wasn't going to share it tonight. And pushing could backfire.

Maybe if he opened up a bit about *his* background, she'd reciprocate.

"My dad's father died when I was very young, so my mom's father was the only grandfather I ever knew. Pop was a great guy." The corners of his mouth ticced up. "He lived in a small town about an hour north of Boston, and he used to take my brother and me sailing every Saturday in the summer. He'd built the boat himself years before. It wasn't big or fancy, but it gave us priceless memories. And I learned a lot from him about self-reliance and initiative and courage. Not a day goes by that I don't miss him."

"What happened to him?"

His lips flattened. "He had a stroke six years ago. Because of bad investments in later years, Pop didn't have much money. My parents and my brother and I all offered him financial help, but he refused. Said he didn't want to be a burden to anyone. Without telling us, he sold his house. Then he moved into an assisted-living facility, where he withered away and died in six months."

"I'm sorry, Christopher." Marci touched the hand he'd balled into a fist.

"So am I."

"That's why you help Henry as much as you do, isn't it?"

"The experience did—"

"Here you go, sweetie." The middle-aged waitress bustled up to the table and slid a plate in front of Marci. "And the special for you, Doc." She set the second plate in front of him. "Enjoy."

Marci removed her hand from his and picked up her fork.

He missed the warmth at once.

"Like I was saying, the experience with my grandfather did give me empathy for the needs of older folks. I'd hate to see Henry end up in the same situation as Pop."

"I thought you said he should be able to go home once he recovers."

"He should—but his daughter will fight it. She's been after him for the past few years to either move into a retirement home on the island or go live with her in Boston. This will give her an excuse to renew that crusade—and in light of his weakened condition, she may wear him down. But his whole life and all his memories are connected to that cottage. Take him away from that, he'll be finished."

"Why is she pushing so hard?"

Christopher speared a broccoli floret. "I've only met her once, but my impression was less than favorable. I think she'd like to sell the cottages. Property on Nantucket is expensive, and Henry's two houses are worth a tidy sum."

"Does she need money?"

"Depends on how you define *need*. She married into wealth, lives in a large home in one of Boston's most desirable neighborhoods, travels quite a bit, wears designer clothes. But I suppose there's always another cruise to take or diamond ring to buy."

Marci frowned. "She and Henry sound like night and day."

"That would be a fair assessment."

"There must be something we can do to override whatever pressure she puts on him. I'm sure we can find a way to help him stay in his house."

The determined set of her chin sent a clear message—Marci Clay could be a force to be reckoned with once she set her mind to a task. "Sounds like Henry has another champion."

"I like him—and I admire independence."

"So do I." He let a beat pass—and a soft flush stole across her cheeks as his message sank in. "Maybe between the two of us we can come up with a plan. But first we have to get him through the next few days."

"I'll do whatever I can to help."

"Good. This may take a team effort. Let's finish up and go pay the patient a visit."

He broke off a bite of his flounder—but though he kept the conversation light for the remainder of the meal, images of Pop kept running through his mind.

Reminding him that no matter how hard they tried to help Henry, in the end the outcome would be in God's hands.

* * *

Twenty minutes later, as Marci approached the door to the recovery room with Christopher, he paused. "Have you been in hospitals much?"

"No."

"Don't let all the equipment disturb you. We'll be keeping a close watch on him for the first day or two."

"Got it."

He pushed the door open and moved aside to let her enter.

Two steps in, she stopped.

Whoa.

Thank heaven Christopher had prepared her.

Henry's bed was surrounded by all sorts of machines emitting odd noises, their digital screens displaying a dizzying array of data.

"This is all routine." Christopher spoke close to her ear, his breath warm on her cheek.

Lucky she wasn't hooked up to the heart monitor blipping out Henry's steady pulse. Her reading would be all over the charts.

She nodded, not trusting her voice.

Christopher's hand in the small of her back urged her forward, and she moved beside Henry's bed.

"How's everything?" Christopher spoke to the nurse on the other side of the room.

"He's doing great."

Henry's eyelids flickered open. "That you, Christopher?"

"Yes. Marci's with me."

She moved into Henry's line of sight. Closer to Christopher. Instead of shifting back, he angled his body until her shoulder brushed his chest. Which did nothing to steady her pulse.

"Hi, Henry."

"You should have gone home, Marci."

"I wanted to stay." She took his hand. "How do you feel? Are you in any pain?"

"Not feeling much of anything at the moment. They must have given me mighty powerful drugs. What time is it?"

Christopher checked his watch. "Eight-thirty."

"Go home. Don't put in any overtime on my account. You too, Marci. The two of you have better things to do than sit around an old man's bedside. And if you don't, you ought to."

"I think we're being kicked out." Christopher rested a hand on her shoulder.

She had to fight the impulse to lean back, against his broad chest. Let his solid strength support her.

But she wasn't a leaner. Never had been. It was safer to stand on your own two feet. To count on no one but yourself.

She bent forward to press a light kiss to Henry's forehead—

and disengage from Christopher's hand. "We get the message, Henry. I'll be back tomorrow."

He gripped her hand and gave it a squeeze. "Thanks for hanging around today. I didn't expect it, but it sure made me feel good." He peered around her. "Why don't you take this pretty lady out for a bite to eat, Christopher?"

"I already did."

Henry's eyebrows rose. "Is that right? Well, maybe there's hope for you yet."

Oh, brother. Henry was as bad as Edith when it came to matchmaking.

Marci rummaged around in her purse. "I guess I'll go home."

"I'll walk you to your car," Christopher offered.

"That's not necessary."

"Always let a gentleman be a gentleman, Marci." This from Henry, who seemed to be enjoying the little drama playing out at his bedside.

"I'm used to taking care of myself."

"Good manners trump independence." Christopher added his voice to Henry's.

She turned to him. "Who says?"

"Letitia Baldridge."

Letitia Baldridge?

Was she an etiquette guru, maybe?

"He's right, Marci." Henry waggled a finger at her.

"Fine." Settling the strap of her purse higher on her shoulder, she edged past him toward the door. Making an issue of it would only raise suspicions. "'Bye, Henry."

"See you later, Marci."

She waited in the hall as the two men had a brief exchange in voices too low to decipher. When Christopher joined her he was smiling.

"He's in excellent spirits tonight. I hope it lasts once his daughter arrives. Where are you parked?"

"Not far from the ER entrance."

He fell into step beside her, and as they exited the building into the deepening twilight, she surveyed the dark clouds overhead. "I think a storm is brewing."

"Yeah. I hope I make it home before it hits."

Her step faltered. "Did you ride your bike to work today?"

"Yes. This"—he swept a hand over the sky—"is one of the downsides of island living. The weather can be changeable. But it won't be the first time I've battled the elements on my bike. Is that your car?" He indicated a late-model compact in the mostly deserted lot.

"Yes." While it would be safer to escape as fast as possible from this all-too-appealing man, letting him bike home with the skies about to open would be wrong. "Look...why don't I give you a lift? You've had a long day."

"You have too—and 'Sconset isn't exactly on your route."

"At this point, adding another twenty or thirty minutes to my day isn't going to make much difference."

"You don't have to strong-arm me. I can drive in tomorrow and pick up my bike before I go to the office. Give me a minute to stow it inside."

As he strode toward the back of the building, Marci leaned against the car and scanned the sky again. Had it remained clear, she would have let Christopher bike home.

But she didn't mind the extra trip to 'Sconset.

Or the extra few minutes with Christopher.

Even if that was a very dangerous sign.

* * *

"We may beat the storm after all." Christopher gave Marci a surreptitious sweep as she focused on the road ahead in the dwindling light. She was tense—and her stress wasn't related to Henry. He'd put money on that.

"Maybe."

"Are you tired?"

She shot him a quick glance. "Why?"

"You're not very talkative."

Twin furrows appeared on her brow. "Sorry. I've been thinking about Henry. He's lucky to have someone like you who cares about him."

"How could I *not* care about him? He's a great guy. You must agree, or you wouldn't be hanging around his place every day."

"I never knew my grandparents. He already sort of feels like one."

"Did they die when you were young?"

"My mom's father died before I was born, and her mother died when I was two. I have no memory of my father's parents—and no good ones of my father." Bitterness etched her voice.

"Is he still living?"

"I don't know. He deserted our family when I was eleven."

That stank.

"I'm sorry, Marci."

She gave a stiff shrug. "Don't be. He drank too much and had a mean streak a mile wide. No one missed him. It was hard on my mom financially, though. She got a second job to make ends meet—until she was killed two years later in a hit-and-run accident. JC ended up raising us while he was practically a kid himself. He did his best, but we lived a bare-bones life in a rough neighborhood for too many years."

No wonder she'd developed a thick skin. "Is your background why you went into social work?"

"Yes. I know what it's like to live in that kind of environment. Trite as it may sound, I'm hoping I can make a difference in someone's life."

"You mentioned *us* earlier. Do you have other siblings besides JC?"

"A brother. Two years older than me." She flexed her fingers on the steering wheel. "So tell me about you, Christopher. Are your parents living? And any siblings besides the brother you referenced?"

The subject of her background was closed for the night.

But he'd learned more than he'd expected.

"Yes. They live in Boston. My brother and his wife and two kids live there too."

"Is that where you lived before you came here?"

"Yes."

"Henry said you've been on the island two years. What brought you here?"

That was *not* a subject he wanted to discuss tonight.

Cracking his window, he took a breath of salty air and chose his words with care. "We always vacationed here for three weeks in the summer when I was a kid. It's a special place for me."

"But didn't you already have an established practice in Boston?" Twin creases dented her brow.

"Yes."

"Are you going to go back?"

"I don't know." His turn to change the subject. "What are your plans for tomorrow?"

She gave him a bemused look. "In other words, butt out?"

"It's a long story—and we've had enough drama for one day."

To his relief, she took his cue as she drove down the quiet streets of 'Sconset and turned onto the byway Henry called home.

Perhaps because she, too, had secrets she didn't want to share?

Secrets he'd like to know.

But unless he shared his, it wasn't fair to ask her to share hers.

And he was nowhere near ready to reveal his shame to anyone—especially a woman who was fast making inroads on his heart, despite his every effort to fortify his defenses.

* * *

After pulling up in front of Henry's cottage, Marci set the brake. "I want to run around the back and get my garden gloves before it rains. I dropped them in the midst of all the excitement."

"I'll go with you. If the birdbath is on the lawn, I can roll it to the side. Henry won't be happy if he finds a dead spot in his grass."

He followed her around back, passing under the fragrant roses on the arbor. Marci picked up her gloves, then walked over to where he was surveying the bowl of the birdbath.

"I can't believe he tried to lift this himself." Christopher planted his fists on his hips. "I've warned him over and over not to take any chances. But he still thinks he's thirty."

"That's probably what keeps him young."

"True—but prudence has to come into play too."

He dropped to one knee, grasped the edge of the bowl, and heaved it upright.

Beneath the rolled-up sleeves of his dress shirt, the muscles in his forearms bunched as he lifted the bowl until it balanced on edge like a wheel. Then he rolled it to the open area that had once housed the gazebo, lowered it to the ground, and returned to her side.

For someone in a sedentary occupation, he was in terrific shape.

"You never answered my question in the car."

"What question?" She tried to refocus.

"About your plans for tomorrow."

"Oh. Uh...I think I'll go see Henry in the morning, then come out here and work for a while. I'll stop by and visit him again on my way home."

"What happened to your beach time?"

She wrinkled her nose. "A little goes a long way. I don't think I have the constitution for sitting around doing nothing."

"Henry told me you put yourself through school working as a waitress." He shoved his hands into his pockets. "It doesn't sound like you've had much downtime in your life."

It was too dim to read his expression—but she had no trouble interpreting his empathetic tone. No one except JC had ever cared how hard she'd worked to reach her goals.

Folding her arms, she quashed a sudden rush of unsettling emotion and turned the tables. "According to Henry, you don't, either."

A gust of wind whipped past, and Marci reached up to push her flyaway hair aside. One of the gloves slipped from her fingers, and she bent to retrieve it.

So did Christopher.

Their hands touched, and her gaze flew to his as a distant

flash of lightning illuminated the sky. At the raw need in those cobalt eyes mere inches away, her lungs locked.

Never in all her thirty-one years had a man sucked her in like this. Not even the man who'd broken her heart.

Slowly, Christopher lifted a hand and brushed her wind-tossed hair back from her face, his fingertips leaving a trail of warmth in their wake. He leaned toward her. She reciprocated. Their lips were inches apart.

And then the heavens opened.

Marci dropped the other glove, sprang to her feet, and stumbled back a few steps. "I'll see you around."

She took off at a run for her car through the deluge.

Only after five minutes and several miles did her pulse begin to return to normal.

But *normal* didn't begin to describe how she felt.

Sweet heaven.

Christopher had almost kissed her.

And she'd almost let him—despite her resolve to be smart. To set a clear limit on a relationship that had no future. Had it not been for the sudden downpour that had put a literal damper on the electricity sparking between them, she might have tossed logic aside and given in to the yearning that had swept over her.

Maybe the shower had been a divine caution sign.

One she should heed.

Because no matter how appealing she found Christopher Morgan, he deserved better than the likes of her.

7

"Back again, huh? Rather see me than eat lunch, I guess."

At Henry's perky greeting and improved color, the tension in Christopher's shoulders dissipated. He nodded toward the large bouquet of flowers on the nightstand. "Pretty."

"Marci brought them."

Why was he not surprised?

"When did she visit?"

"Came about fifteen minutes ago. She ran out to refill my water pitcher."

She was still here?

Blast.

After that charged moment in Henry's backyard last night, they needed to give the sparks a chance to subside before another encounter. Maybe he could escape before—

"You're set, Henry. I filled—"

Too late.

As Marci's unfinished sentence hung in the air, Christopher turned toward the door.

She was hovering on the threshold as if debating whether to bolt.

"Come on in, Marci. You can set that next to the flowers you brought."

Her gaze darted to his before she edged around the far side of the bed to deposit the pitcher.

Henry's head swiveled between the two of them. "Something going on here I don't know about?"

Christopher hiked up the corners of his mouth. "Heightened imagination can be an aftereffect of the anesthesia." He angled toward Marci. "Are you going to work on the garden today?"

"Yes. That's my next stop—and I'm running way behind." She picked up her purse. "I'll come by on my way home, Henry. And you have my cell number. I'll keep the phone in my pocket."

"I'll be fine. This is a first-class operation. Thanks again for the flowers. You didn't have to spend your money on me."

A dimple appeared in her cheek. "In the interest of full transparency, I didn't. I raided my sister-in-law's garden and—"

"Could someone please direct me to Henry Calhoun's room?"

As the imperious voice echoed down the hall outside Henry's room, the older man closed his eyes and gave a slight groan. "Let the games begin."

At Marci's telegraphed question, Christopher mouthed the answer.

His daughter.

Five seconds later, when Patricia Lawrence made her entrance, Christopher gave her a quick sweep.

She hadn't changed much in the past year. Same short hairstyle. Same flawless makeup. Same chic, designer clothes that couldn't hide the extra twenty pounds on her fifty-year-old frame. She did seem a bit younger. Could be Botox or a filler.

Patricia's eyes narrowed when she saw Marci, though she ignored the younger woman.

"Is he sleeping?" She scrutinized her father.

Henry opened his eyes. "No, Patricia, he isn't sleeping."

Her lips thinned. "Hello, Dad. Dr. Morgan." She nodded at him, then addressed Marci. "I don't believe we've met."

Henry took care of the introductions.

Marci moved toward the end of the bed and extended her hand. "Nice to meet you."

After a tiny hesitation, the woman leaned over and took it—but didn't return the sentiment.

"I'd like to hear about my father's condition, Doctor." She shot Marci a pointed look. "Is there somewhere private we could speak?"

A flush suffused Marci's face, but before she could respond, Henry chimed in.

"You can speak right here. I have a right to hear whatever is said. And if it wasn't for Marci, I might still be lying in the yard with that birdbath on top of me. Plus, she spent most of yesterday keeping vigil in the ER. She can hear anything Christopher has to say."

Bright spots of color appeared on Patricia's cheeks. "Fine. Doctor?"

As Christopher briefed her, he kept tabs on Marci in his peripheral vision. She'd backed as close to the wall as she could get in the confined space and was fidgeting with her purse. It was all he could do to maintain a cool, professional tone despite his anger at Patricia for making Marci feel uncomfortable—and unwelcome.

"When will he be released?" Patricia tapped her foot as he finished.

"If he continues to do well, in four or five days."

"How much help will he need after that?"

"Quite a bit for the first week to ten days."

"In that case, we'll have to arrange for assisted living." She tucked her Coach purse under her arm. "I certainly can't stay that long. I have commitments in Boston. I'm chairing a fundraiser for the zoo a week from tomorrow, and the preceding few days will be crazy."

"I'm not going into assisted living, Patricia."

At Henry's pronouncement, her lips turned down. "Don't be stubborn, Dad. This is the best solution."

"For you, maybe."

She glared at him. "You make it sound as if I'm selfish."

"If the shoe fits…"

"Well." She sniffed. "That's a fine thing to say after I came all the way down here from Boston. Do you realize I had to be at the airport at seven this morning? I never even get up until eight. And I'm missing a dinner party tonight that's very important to Jonathan's career so I could be with you. Plus, I had to rearrange my entire schedule for Monday to accommodate this trip. My hairdresser was *not* pleased. How in the world can you call that selfish?"

Henry closed his eyes, as if suddenly weary. "I rest my case."

"Dad, we're not through discussing this."

"Yes, we are—for today." Christopher moved to the foot of the bed and motioned for her to precede him into the hall. Waited until she did, then followed her out. "Your father isn't up to a debate. We can work out the details of his recuperation over the next few days. How long are you staying?"

"I planned to leave Monday night."

"We'll figure everything out by then. For now, your father needs rest. Short visits are best."

"What about *her?*" The woman waved a manicured hand toward the room.

"She'll be leaving in a moment too."

Patricia adjusted her jacket and smoothed her hair. "Very well. I came straight here from the airport, and I need to freshen up anyway. You can reach me at The Wauwinet or on my cell. Dad has the number."

Without giving him a chance to respond, she marched down the hall, heels tapping a staccato rhythm.

"Wow." At Marci's soft comment, Christopher turned as she peeked out of the room. "How in the world did Henry end up with a daughter like her?"

"To hear Henry tell it, Patricia was always a social climber. He thinks it was because she saw a lot of wealth in 'Sconset among the summer people, and it made her dissatisfied with their simple lifestyle." He propped his shoulder against the wall and crossed his arms. "According to him, she set her sights on marrying into money—and she succeeded. She landed a rich guy who vacationed in 'Sconset every year with his family while he was growing up."

"Does she have any children?"

"No. Patricia is all the family Henry's got."

"I overheard her mention a hotel. I take it she doesn't stay at the cottage when she visits?"

"No. It's not up to her standards." He straightened and motioned toward the room. "Let's say goodbye."

When they reentered, Henry partially opened one eye. "Is she gone?"

"For now."

"She's gonna keep pushing for that old-folks home, you know." Henry sighed. "Too bad you never got that elder-assistance program off the ground."

"The what?" Marci stopped beside Henry's bed.

"Tell her about it, Christopher."

He shoved his hands into his pockets. "The concept is to set up an on-island agency that would coordinate assistance from a network of government, private, and charitable groups to allow older folks who need a little help to stay in their homes. There are a number of resources already out there, and more could be developed. I envisioned it as a largely volunteer organization supported by area churches, businesses, and civic groups."

"That's a great idea."

"I told him the same thing," Henry chimed in.

"I agree it has potential. Unfortunately, working out the details of the plan and then implementing it will require a ton of legwork, and I'm already stretched thin. It's never gotten past the drawing-board stage."

"Maybe someday." Henry's eyelids drifted closed.

Inclining his head toward the door, Christopher waited for Marci to take the cue, then followed her out.

"I left your gloves under the cushion of the rocking chair on the back porch. They should have stayed dry, despite the rain."

The potent awareness between them ratcheted up again.

"Thanks. I'll, uh, see you around." Without waiting for a reply, she sped toward the exit.

Running away from the high-voltage attraction.

As she disappeared around a corner, Christopher followed. He should pick up his pace too. He had another full patient load today, courtesy of his growing practice.

But as he walked down the hall, the colds and tick bites and sore throats and allergies he'd be treating for the rest of the day weren't top of mind. Those problems he could handle.

The problems of what to do about an elderly man he'd come

to love and a blond-haired woman who was beginning to make her own inroads on his heart, however?

Those were far less easy to solve.

* * *

"What are you doing here?"

Marci gasped and spun around, scattering an armful of weeds. After three peaceful hours in Henry's garden, with only the sound of the gulls and the surf for company, the strident voice was like the crash of a dissonant chord in one of those avant-garde compositions Preston had liked.

Patricia stood on the other side of the rose arbor—and she didn't seem happy.

Planting her fists on her hips, Marci regarded the other woman. "Working in the garden."

"I can see that. My question is *why?*"

Her chin lifted a notch at the woman's snippy attitude. "Actually, your question was *what*. I answered that one. As for why, the garden needed tending. I offered to help Henry with it."

Patricia's eye twitched. "How much is he paying you?"

"I'm not doing it for money."

Stay calm, Marci.

"Then what *are* you doing it for?" The woman's gaze raked over her. "And just who are you, anyway?"

Marci ignored the first part of the question. "I'm a friend of Henry's."

His daughter's face hardened. "Do you have a key to the house?"

That question didn't merit a response.

"If you'll excuse me, I have work to do." She turned her

back, retrieved the rake, and began to gather the scattered weeds into a pile.

Three minutes later, a car engine started. Tires crunched on oyster shells as the woman departed.

Thank heaven.

Leaning on the rake, Marci took a deep breath. How could that obnoxious woman share Henry's DNA?

And why had she come to the cottage? To assess its condition—with the intention of selling? Christopher had said she'd like to oust Henry, put the house on the market, and perhaps claim an early share of her inheritance.

Marci set the rake aside and began shoving weeds into a yard-waste bag.

It might come to that someday—but it didn't have to happen now. Not if Henry had help until he recovered.

She had three weeks left on the island—and a ton of free time.

Why not use it to thwart Patricia's plans?

* * *

Henry was asleep when Marci stopped in at the hospital later that day, but by the next morning she was prepared to lay out a plan for his return to his cottage.

As she drew close to his room, however, Patricia's insistent voice echoed down the hallway.

"Dad, be reasonable. Your pension from the high school and the money you make tutoring aren't enough to get you the kind of in-home help you'll need. Face reality. You're old. You're hurt. You need to go into an assisted-living facility. It's time to sell the houses."

"I'm not leaving the cottage, Patricia."

Squaring her shoulders, Marci stepped into the room. Henry's face lit up when he saw her, and Patricia swiveled around.

His daughter's expression was far less welcoming.

"Excuse me, Dad. I think I'll visit the ladies' room. It's getting crowded in here."

She swept toward the door, and Marci stepped aside to let her pass.

"Come on in, Marci." Henry summoned her with a weary wave. "I'm sorry about Patricia. Her mother and I raised her better than that. But my refusal to sell the cottages has her in a snit. I never could figure out why she put such stock in the almighty dollar."

Marci pulled a chair beside the bed and sat. "I've been thinking, Henry. We'll have to see what Christopher says, but I'll be here for three more weeks. If that's long enough to get you over the hump, I'd be happy to help you out at the cottage. That way you wouldn't have to go to the assisted-living place."

Moisture glinted at the corners of his eyes as he reached out to take her hand. "That's a very generous offer."

She shrugged. "I'm at the cottage every day anyway, working on the garden. And I'm tired of lying on the beach. We may be able to put together a plan."

He brightened. "I like the idea. Let's see what Christopher says about it. I'll talk to him when he comes by later."

After patting his hand, Marci rose. "That patch of weeds in the right corner is on my hit list today. You won't believe all the beautiful flowers that are emerging."

"I can't wait to see them."

"Do you need anything before I leave?"

"You already gave me what I needed most. Hope."

With a thumbs-up, Marci stepped through the door...and found Patricia glaring at her.

The woman pointed to her, then down the hall, and stalked away.

Should she ignore the haughty summons?

No.

She'd have to deal with Henry's daughter at some point. Safer to do it here, with other people around, than risk another encounter in the privacy of Henry's backyard. At least with witnesses close by the woman might be more civil.

Marci followed Patricia into the deserted waiting room.

The woman rounded on her, fury contorting her features. "I heard what you said about caring for my father at the cottage. Why are you butting into his life?"

"I want what's best for him. He's my friend."

"A very *new* friend, according to Dad. He told me last night you only met a couple of weeks ago—and that you're a visitor who will be leaving next month. I also learned you're a waitress. Not the best-paying profession."

Marci gritted her teeth. "I'm not a waitress anymore."

"Nevertheless...I can see where the opportunity to make an easy buck could be appealing." She gave Marci's jeans and T-shirt a snooty scan. "But don't waste your time. My father may own valuable property, but he isn't wealthy. He is, however, a gullible man who tends to think the best of people and is therefore vulnerable to exploitation."

Exploitation?

Anger began to churn in her gut.

"I don't like your insinuations. I'm helping Henry because I like him. Period."

"If you liked him, you wouldn't have let him do physical work. He's eighty-five years old. That fall could have killed him. And it wouldn't have happened if you hadn't pushed him to clean up the garden."

A wave of guilt crashed over her.

Was his accident her fault? If she hadn't offered to—

"Good morning, ladies."

Patricia twisted around, acknowledging Christopher's presence with a stiff nod. "Doctor."

"I couldn't help overhearing some of your conversation." Though his tone was calm, his eyes were turbulent as he moved beside her in a protective stance and addressed Henry's daughter. "I can assure you, Ms. Lawrence, that Henry was eager to restore order to his garden. He didn't have to be pushed. But as you know, he tends to overextend himself."

"That's exactly why I want him in a place with professional oversight. Despite Ms. Clay's…generous…offer of assistance, I don't believe she has the appropriate medical credentials to care for my father. Do you, Doctor?"

"I do agree that a short-term stay at an extended-care facility is advisable—but if he improves as I expect him to, he should be able to return to his cottage. And that will be far better for his psychological well-being long-term."

A wave of nausea swept over Marci.

Christopher had nixed her plan before she could even present it. Worse, he'd betrayed Henry.

Ignoring Patricia, she tightened her grip on the strap of her purse and brushed past him. "If you'll excuse me, I have another commitment."

Fighting back tears, she strode down the hall.

How could Christopher do this? He knew Henry didn't want

to go into assisted living. Yes, he'd said it would be a short-term stay—but from what she'd seen of Patricia, the woman could sell the cottage out from under Henry while he was away.

She pushed through the door to the ladies' room, swiping at the tear that spilled past her lower lashes. What would happen to Henry if Patricia won this skirmish?

The possibilities weren't pretty.

So she'd hide here for a few minutes. Pull herself together. Muster her chutzpah.

And then she'd go into battle mode.

* * *

As Christopher turned the corner in the hall where Marci had disappeared, she entered the ladies' room.

He continued to the door, leaned against the opposite wall, and shoved his hands into his pockets. Patricia would be waiting for him in her father's room to discuss next steps, but Marci was his top priority after that flash of gut-twisting betrayal in her eyes before she'd bolted.

Three minutes later, when the door opened and she emerged, he straightened up. Given the mutinous tilt of her chin, what he had to say was going to be a hard sell.

"I expected you to be busy with Patricia arranging Henry's move to assisted living." She positioned her purse in front of her like a shield, her splotchy face clear evidence she'd been crying.

"I'm not selling him out."

She glared at him. "You could have fooled me."

"I'll explain if you give me a chance." He motioned to an adjacent door marked private.

She hesitated...then walked over to it. Twisted the knob. "This is a supply closet."

"Any port in a storm." He urged her inside with slight pressure in the small of her back and closed the door.

She spun around. "You know he doesn't want to go to assisted living. You said yourself he'd wither and die in a place like that, just like your grandfather did."

"That's true. But I also saw the results of his latest tests this morning. His blood count isn't rebounding as fast as we'd like—and he's having a lot more discomfort than he's letting on to visitors. That should all improve...but it will take a while. For the first week or so, I'll feel more comfortable if he's got round-the-clock care from medical professionals. After that, assuming we can arrange for home help, he can return to the cottage."

"If his daughter doesn't sell it in the meantime."

"She can't do that. I have his power of attorney."

A few beats passed as she processed that. Then the tension in her features and stance eased.

"In other words, Henry trusts you more than he does his own daughter." She blew out a breath. "I guess I overreacted. Sorry about that."

"Don't apologize for caring. His daughter could take a few lessons from you."

"I just don't like to see people being used."

The sudden hard edge to her words raised his antennas—and his protective instincts. "Neither do I. It's especially troubling if you've been on the receiving end of that kind of treatment." He'd given her an ideal opening—if she wanted to talk.

She didn't take it.

"I suppose that's true. Plus, I do feel a bit guilty. As Patricia pointed out, if I hadn't convinced him to fix up the garden, this wouldn't have happened." Her irises began to shimmer.

He clenched his jaw. The caring woman standing inches away deserved gratitude, not insults. "Henry's been wanting to clean it out for months. He was thrilled by your offer of help. Don't let her lay a guilt trip on you." He propped a shoulder against the closed door. "Are you going to Henry's now?"

"That was my plan—but with this new turn of events, I think I'll go back to The Devon Rose and see if I can borrow Heather's computer. As part of my last social-work practicum, I helped find assistance for seniors. I want to search the net and see what I can come up with for Henry. I'd also like to see your elder-assistance plan, if you're willing to share it. It may spark a few ideas."

"You're welcome to read it—but be warned it's rough. I keep it at my office." He folded his arms. "You know, our office manager isn't there on Saturdays. You could come by and not only get the plan, but use her computer for research."

"Are you sure I wouldn't disrupt anything?"

Only his heart.

"No. Let me finish up with Henry, and I'll meet you there in about fifteen minutes. It's easy to find." He pulled out a prescription pad, jotted down the directions, and tore off the sheet.

After a quick skim, she tucked it in the pocket of her jeans. Waited for him to open the door.

Which he should do.

But it was hard to move when a whisper of yearning stirred to life in her emerald irises.

She moistened her lips.

His gaze dropped to their soft fullness...and his pulse stumbled.

Get out of here, Morgan. A hospital supply closet isn't the place to be entertaining the kind of thoughts that can short-circuit sound judgment.

He fumbled for the knob behind him and pulled the door open. "I'll, uh, see you in a few minutes."

Her breath hitched…and she edged past him. Took off down the hall at a fast clip. Disappeared around a corner.

He let out a slow breath. That had been close.

But not close enough.

For while he may have regretted succumbing to the temptation to taste her lips in that most unromantic and inappropriate setting—there would have been no regrets about the kiss itself.

Because the more he got to know Marci, the less she reminded him of Denise. The woman who'd upended his life had used tears to get what she wanted. Marci did her best to hide hers. Denise had been needy. Marci reached out to those in need. She was also smart, intelligent, spunky, kind, attractive.

The big unknown was why some guy hadn't claimed her by now.

Had the secrets she harbored given her an aversion to romance?

An important question—for both of them.

And he needed to find the answer before she boarded a plane to Chicago in three weeks and disappeared from his life forever.

8

This was great stuff.

Marci tapped Christopher's notes on the elder-assistance program into a neat stack, slid them into the file, and leaned back in the office manager's chair.

While he'd claimed to have done little, that wasn't quite true. He'd made a number of contacts in the community, and his idea had been met with a positive response. He'd compiled a list of contacts yet to be tapped. And he'd researched some of the services already available to seniors on Nantucket. It was an excellent start.

After setting aside the file, Marci began browsing the net.

By the time the receptionist appeared in the doorway of the small office, she'd found several additional resources for seniors that sounded worthy of investigation, along with a number of interesting articles about new programs sprouting up around the country designed around the philosophy of keeping older citizens in their homes.

"Sorry to interrupt. I wanted to let you know we'll be closing at one. I thought you might need a few minutes to wrap up."

Marci twisted her wrist. Did a double take at her watch. Where had the past three hours gone?

"Thanks. I'm about done anyway. Would you like me to shut down the computer?"

"I'll take care of it. And don't feel you have to rush. Dr. Morgan still has a patient in the waiting room."

"Thanks."

After the woman left, Marci finished jotting a few notes about an innovative time-bank idea, tucked Christopher's file into the crook of her arm, and stood. It had been a productive morning.

The receptionist was at her desk when Marci emerged. The woman motioned to the file as she approached. "It's a great idea, isn't it?"

"Yes. It could help a lot of people." She left it at that in case Christopher hadn't shared details of the plan with his office staff.

"My own grandmother, for one. She's seventy-nine and has lived in the same house since she got married fifty-eight years ago. But it's getting to be too much for her to manage. I know she'd—"

A baby's wail pierced the air from the direction of the waiting room as one of the examining-room doors opened. A smock-clad nurse with salt-and-pepper hair stepped into the hall, closing the door behind her. "I take it Mrs. Carter has arrived."

"With brood in tow." The receptionist sighed.

"At least it's the last patient of the day." The nurse grinned and walked to the door, ushering in a young mother who was bouncing the screaming baby. The toddler clinging to the woman's skirt gave the adults in the office a wary inspection.

"Let's get your weight." The nurse doubled her volume to be heard above the howling infant and indicated the scale in the hall near the reception desk.

The baby gave another piercing wail as the woman tried to shrug the slipping diaper bag back onto her shoulder.

"If this keeps up, I'll be having hearing problems too."

Marci offered her a sympathetic smile—and the young mother flashed her a grin. "Would you mind holding my baby while I get weighed? I don't need the extra fourteen pounds."

Before Marci could protest, she placed the flailing infant in her arms.

As the squirming little body settled against her chest, Marci stared down at the scrunched-up face.

And tried to breathe.

"Here, let me help. Your arms are full." The receptionist stood and leaned over the desk to relieve her of Christopher's file and her notes. "Isn't she a cutie, with those red curls?" She touched the baby's nose.

"Danny, let go of Mommy's skirt. She has to get on the scale." The mother was still trying to disengage from her toddler.

The infant continued to scream, and Marci began to bounce her.

"This baby is one of Dr. Morgan's special children." The receptionist rested her arms on the desk and regarded the little bundle.

The tiny warm body squirmed against her chest, and Marci tightened her stiff arms. "What do you mean?"

"He's very active in the pro-life movement. Mrs. Carter couldn't have any more children after Danny, but she wanted another baby. Dr. Morgan helped arrange an adoption through his connections with Birthright in Boston."

A film of sweat broke out on her upper lip.

The receptionist inspected the baby in her arms. "You must have the touch. Peace reigns once again."

Marci looked down.

The infant was staring up at her with big blue eyes, one fist jammed in her mouth. With the other hand, she grabbed a fistful of Marci's T-shirt and hiccupped.

As the diminutive fist held tight, Marci stopped breathing. Each finger was so tiny, yet so perfect. Just like—

A door opened down the hall, and a few seconds later a white-coated Christopher joined the small group gathered by the receptionist's desk.

Legs wooden, Marci crossed to him in the suddenly airless room. "I have to g-go." She pushed the baby against his chest.

He frowned—but lifted his arms.

Once the baby was secure, she turned away and rushed to the door, fumbling with the knob.

"Marci, wait a second. What's the—"

She didn't pause to hear the rest of his question. Instead, she pushed through the door, dashed across the empty waiting room—and ran to her car.

Once behind the wheel, she fitted the key into the ignition, fighting back sobs—and a heaping dose of embarrassment over what everyone in that office must have deemed bizarre behavior.

But it wasn't. Not if you knew what had prompted it.

Only two people were privy to that secret, however.

And Marci had no intention of revealing it to anyone else.

* * *

As Christopher approached 'Sconset, he eased back on the accelerator.

Maybe he should have followed through on his original plan to visit Henry again after finishing at the office.

But he had to get to the bottom of Marci's hasty departure—and distraught demeanor—and his receptionist hadn't been able to offer any clues about what had upset her.

Yet something had.

Big time.

Of course, this could be a wasted trip. She could have gone home after she left his office. If she'd answered her phone, he'd know for certain.

But she'd let it roll—leading him here. If she was seeking a quiet place to think through whatever had upset her, the private garden she'd adopted as her own seemed the logical place.

Her car came into view as he pulled onto Henry's street, parked near the arbor in the older man's backyard, and he released the breath he hadn't realized he'd been holding.

His hunch had been spot-on.

He parked in front of his cottage, entered through the front door, and strode toward the window in his tiny kitchenette.

Hoe in hand, Marci was attacking the weeds with a vengeance.

Her heads-down, yank-those-suckers-out manner suggested she wasn't about to quit anytime soon. That should give him a chance to exchange his work clothes for jeans and a T-shirt.

He made the swap as fast as he could, picked up the elder-assistance file and notes she'd left in his office, and slipped through the back door. The lush grass muffled his approach as he walked to the picket fence that separated the two yards.

"Could you use a hand?"

At his question, Marci swung toward him, hoe frozen midstrike. "I thought you said you were going to do rounds after office hours?"

"I changed my mind. I'm filling in for half a shift in the ER tonight, so I'll visit patients before that." He waved the file and papers at her. "You left these behind."

A faint pink tinge crept over her cheeks as she set the hoe

aside and approached him. "Sorry." She reached across the fence to take them.

He tightened his grip. "Before I hand these over, do you want to tell me what happened back at the office?"

She retracted her hand and tucked it in her pocket, features neutral. "What do you mean?"

"You know what I mean. You were upset."

She lifted one shoulder, her nonchalance too deliberate to be authentic. "I was still thinking about the encounter with Henry's daughter."

That was a lie.

But maybe if he could put her at ease, she'd open up.

He waved the file and notes, and she drew close again. Took them.

When he vaulted the fence, she scuttled back. "Patricia can do that to a person." He kept his tone conversational. "I had to bite my tongue more than once while she and I and Henry discussed his recuperation plans."

"How did he take the news about going to the assisted-living place?"

"Not well. I hope when we talk one-on-one he'll realize it's for the best in the short-term."

"Good luck." She walked over to the porch and deposited her notes and the file on the rocking chair in the corner.

"Yeah. So..." He scanned the yard. "Tell me where you could use an extra pair of hands."

She gave him a wary once-over. "Why do you want to help in the garden?"

"This day's too beautiful to waste indoors."

"Do you know how to tell weeds and flowers apart?"

"I think so—but I may need a bit of coaching."

After a moment, she swept a hand over the long expanse by the fence on the far side of the yard. "I'm working on that section this afternoon."

"Lead the way."

After a momentary hesitation, she complied.

He fell in behind her. It was cute how her springy blond curls bounced when she walked. And the view of her trim figure wasn't too shabby, either. She also moved with an inherent grace that—

"Well?" She swiveled toward him.

Uh-oh.

"Sorry. I was, uh, thinking about how sunny it is. With your fair skin, you should be wearing a hat." A partially true statement. The long hours in the sun *had* brought out a faint sprinkling of freckles across the bridge of her nose.

"I use a ton of sunscreen." She pointed to a section of the garden. "I asked if you want to start here."

"That's fine."

"If you have any questions, ask. I don't want you pulling up half of Henry's flowers."

She moved a few feet down, dropped to her knees, and dove in.

Now that he was up close and personal with the overgrown garden, the scope of the task was a mite intimidating. "Wow. This is a mess."

"Tell me about it."

He began yanking out weeds. "Are you sorry you took on the challenge?"

"No. Neglected gardens are sad. It cheers me up to give the flowers an environment where they can thrive and bloom."

"You're making huge progress." Near as he could tell after a quick scan, she was three-fourths of the way through.

"It's coming along. I want it to be done when Henry comes home." She shoved her hair back from her face, leaving a streak of dirt on her cheek. "I was very impressed with your elder-assistance plan."

"It's rough."

"You've laid a solid foundation, though. And you've identified an impressive number of potential supporters and resources. I like the idea of a talent-exchange registry. It would offer services not available through existing programs like meals-on-wheels and the island shuttle."

He gently extricated a daisy from a tangle of greenery and began pulling up the weeds that were choking it. "It has potential—but it's not a new concept. Bartering has been around for ages. This just formalizes it. For example, Henry taught English for years. He could help someone polish their résumé, or review a college-application essay, or help draft a grant for a local nonprofit organization. They, in turn, could paint his house…or weed his garden…or run errands."

"Building on that idea, I read about a couple of groups that are also doing time banks, where seniors help each other. For every hour they help someone else—whether it's caring for a pet, grocery shopping, changing light bulbs, raking leaves, you name it—they bank hours they can redeem for help when they need it." She'd stopped pulling weeds, her eyes were sparkling with enthusiasm—and she was flat-out gorgeous, despite her tangled hair and dirty face and grubby clothes.

Because her true beauty came from within.

Her lips parted slightly under his appreciative perusal—and she froze as an electrical storm began to swirl around them.

He had to diffuse the tension or she'd retreat.

Yanking his gaze away, he resumed weeding. If a few posies

bit the dust instead of weeds because of his distraction, so be it. "I like the concept of a time bank."

After a couple of seconds, she went back to work too. "What I like best about those kinds of approaches is that no one feels like they're relying on charity or taking advantage of someone else. We could even pull in young people. Maybe for each half hour they volunteer, they could earn points redeemable for merchandise or movies or food donated by area businesses. Plus, I think interaction between seniors and young people would be a positive. Older folks are often an untapped resource in our society."

"I agree with everything you've said—but launching a project like that would be a huge time commitment. That's why it's never gotten off the ground."

She surveyed the garden. "I'll have this done in another few days. If you like, I could at least get the ball rolling while I'm lining up resources for Henry."

"Fine by me. With my packed schedule, I'm never going to be able to make it a reality."

"I'll start by getting in touch with the contacts you listed. Any suggestions on who to talk to first?"

"Reverend Kaizer, at my church. I mentioned the idea to him months ago, and he was very supportive. Plus, he's well-connected on the island. He could put you in touch with people who may be willing to help. I'd be happy to introduce you to him if you'd like to join me for services tomorrow."

She froze for an instant...then resumed tugging at a stubborn weed. "I'm not a churchgoer. God and I have never communicated much." There was a hint of poignancy in her voice.

"It sounds like you wish that would change."

"Sometimes. JC finds great solace in his faith. Even my other brother, who was never interested in religion, has embraced the concept. But I'm not exactly a role model for Christianity." She rubbed her palms on her jeans, leaving streaks of dirt on the fabric.

"I find that hard to believe."

"Believe it." The firm set of her jaw sent a strong back-off message.

He took the cue. "No matter why you believe that, I can promise that you'd be welcome at my church. And it would give you a chance to meet Reverend Kaizer."

There was silence for a few moments as she dug in the fertile earth. "I'll think about it."

"Deal." At least she hadn't refused outright. "Is this ferny stuff a flower?"

She crawled closer to inspect it. Close enough for him to get a whiff of her sweet scent. Close enough to feel the heat emanating from her body. Close enough to find himself fighting the impulse to lift his hand and touch those golden curls.

"That's an astilbe. They get colored plumes later in the summer—or so Henry tells me."

She crawled back and continued her work.

Over the next hour, Christopher introduced several other topics—but Marci clammed up.

Finally he rose. "I have to eat dinner and take care of a few items on my to-do list before I go back to town."

She stood as well, brushing off the knees of her jeans. "I'm about to call it a day too."

"I'll help you clean up."

Once the garden tools were stored in Henry's shed, Marci went to retrieve her purse and the file and notes from the chair on the porch.

MEANT FOR EACH OTHER

"I'm going to go home and change." She dug around in her purse and withdrew her keys. "Would you tell Henry I'll stop by later?"

"Sure. Let me give you my cell number. You can call and tell me what you decide about church. I'll have my phone with me in the ER."

She pulled out her phone and entered the numbers as he recited them. "Thanks for helping today."

"It was a pleasure." He surveyed the view over the fence at the back of Henry's property, where grass gave way to sand and the sea sparkled in the sun. "I don't often have the opportunity to spend an impromptu hour or two outside on a beautiful day. It was a treat."

"I hear you. This spot feels like a little piece of heaven." A winsome smile tugged at Marci's lips as she, too, admired the view, the golden afternoon light warming the hue of her porcelain skin. "See you later." With a wave, she strolled toward the gate.

He remained in the garden until the wheels of her car crunched in front of the cottage, signaling her departure.

Yet her faint, sweet scent lingered.

Along with a deep yearning that was getting harder to control by the day.

9

This was a mistake.

As Marci flipped through the small closet in her cottage trying to find a suitable outfit for church, a tsunami of second thoughts crashed over her.

She did *not* belong in a house of God.

But she did want to meet the minister. Christopher had said the man was enthusiastic about the elder-assistance idea—and if she was going to pull anything together in the short time she had left on the island, she needed all the help she could get.

God would have to put up with her for one day.

Settling on a beige skirt and cotton madras blouse, she pulled them off their hangers as a knock sounded at the door.

Her pulse took a leap.

Why was Christopher twenty minutes early? She wasn't anywhere close to ready.

"Marci?" Another knock. "You there?"

She sagged against the wall. JC.

"Hang on." She pushed herself upright, padded over to the door, and pulled it open.

Her brother grinned as he inspected her baggy sleep shirt, tousled curls, and bare feet. "Did I wake you?"

"It's eight-thirty. Only slugs sleep this late."

"Sleeping late is allowed on vacation. Although this hasn't been much of one for you, from what I can see."

"I like to keep busy."

"That's not what vacation is supposed to be all about."

She folded her arms. "To each his own. What's up?"

"A bit prickly this morning, aren't we?"

Instead of replying, she arched a disparaging eyebrow—a well-practiced technique that discouraged most men.

It didn't work with her brother. Never had.

Grin still in place, he propped a shoulder against the doorframe. "You know, I love you even when you're in one of these ornery moods. Anyway, Heather and I are going to brunch after church. Want to join us? We could swing back around and pick you up."

Uh-oh.

Her plan to surprise him at church so he'd have the whole service to recover from his shock before confronting her was toast. And Heather wasn't around now, as she would have been after the service, to rein in the interrogation.

"Um, I don't think that will work."

"Why not? We'll have the car, so you can't go anywhere. You may as well eat with us."

She was stuck.

Gripping the edge of the door, she spilled it. "I don't know what my plans will be after church. I'm going to the service with Christopher."

JC's face went blank. "You're going to church?"

"Yes."

"With Christopher Morgan? Henry's neighbor?"

"Yes."

"Why?"

"To meet the minister. He may be willing to help get the elder-assistance program I told you about off the ground—and that will benefit Henry." She tapped her watch. "My ride will be here in a few minutes. I have to get ready."

She started to close the door, but JC's hand shot out and grabbed it. "Not so fast. You can't drop a bombshell like that and then shut me out. I've been trying for years to get you to go to church. Yet Morgan invites you, and you accept. Why do I think there's more to this than helping Henry?"

"Because you have a suspicious and cynical mind honed by years of detective work among the dregs of Chicago humanity." She shook the door as heat crept across her cheeks. "Let it go, JC—and I'm talking about more than the door."

He ignored her. "You're blushing. Am I sensing a touch of romance here?"

"Just because you're a newlywed does not mean others share your interest in all that mushy stuff."

"Sounds like a certain 'Sconset doctor might."

She clamped her lips together, jerked the door free, and slammed it in his face.

His muted laughter seeped through the wood. "For the record, I'm all for it."

"Goodbye, JC."

Another chuckle. "See you at church."

The sound of his off-key whistling floated in through the open window as he sauntered back down the flagstone path toward Lighthouse Lane.

Brothers!

Marci stomped into the bathroom, rummaged through her makeup kit, and twisted the cap off her mascara.

JC was reading way too much into this church visit. Christopher had only suggested they attend services together so he could introduce her to the minister. There had been nothing personal about the invitation.

Get real, Marci. A simple phone call to the minister would have sufficed as an introduction. He invited you for the same reason you accepted—and you know what that is.

She recapped her mascara. Sighed.

Yeah, she did.

While she'd consented to accompany Christopher on the pretext of implementing his plan and helping Henry, attraction to the blue-eyed doctor with the compassionate heart had been a key factor in her decision.

And based on that moment in the garden when he'd almost kissed her, before the rain dampened his ardor, the feeling was mutual.

That was the truth of it. Straight-up. And ignoring the reality wasn't going to change it. She had to be honest with herself.

However, that honesty did *not* have to extend to her brother.

Because the last thing she needed in her life was another matchmaker.

* * *

As the pianist played the introduction for the final hymn, Christopher peeked at Marci. Although she'd seemed a bit on edge when he'd picked her up, her expression now was serene, suggesting she'd found the experience worthwhile.

And that was heartening on a number of fronts—some of them personal. Including the fact that it was much less complicated to date a woman who shared his basic beliefs.

Not that this was a date—even if he wished it was.

The hymn ended, and Christopher stepped out of the pew. When Marci exited behind him, he took her arm and guided her toward the back of church. "What did you think?"

"It was interesting. I didn't expect to leave with such a peaceful feeling. Is it like that for you?"

"Every Sunday."

As they joined the groups of congregants gathering on the church lawn, Edith waved to them, took Chester's arm, and tugged him their direction.

"Well, isn't this cozy!" She beamed at them as she drew close. "I didn't realize you two were so well acquainted."

At Marci's blush, Christopher diverted the conversation to a less personal topic. "Marci's working on that elder-assistance program I mentioned to you a few months ago. She may want to tap into your network of contacts."

"Glad to help. It's a worthwhile effort. What got you interested, Marci?"

"Henry Calhoun, Christopher's neighbor. He had a fall, and he'll need assistance once he goes home. I met him when he came to tea, and we hit it off."

Edith tut-tutted. "I heard about Henry's accident from a friend who works at the hospital. Don't know him well myself, but we've exchanged pleasantries on a few occasions. A very agreeable man. You've met him, haven't you, Chester?"

"Yep."

Christopher took Marci's arm—a proprietary gesture not lost on Edith, judging by the sudden twinkle in the older woman's eye. "If you'll excuse us, I want to introduce Marci to Reverend Kaizer. He'll be another invaluable resource for the program."

"By all means. Catch him while he has a free minute. See you both later." With a flutter of fingers, Edith took off toward another cluster of people, Chester trotting along a few steps behind.

"She's a dynamo." Marci followed her progress across the lawn.

"No grass grows under her feet, that's for sure." He motioned toward the minister. "Let's catch Reverend Kaizer before someone else corners him."

Five minutes later, after a conversation that included setting up an appointment for Marci to meet with the man early in the week, Christopher strolled beside her across the grass toward his car. "I stopped in to see Henry on my way to pick you up."

"I'm planning to visit him later. How is he?" Marci brushed back a few wayward strands of hair that were misbehaving in the capricious wind.

"Improving. When I left, he was trying to convince Patricia to go back to Boston early."

"I can't say I blame him. She's—"

"Marci!"

At the summons from Marci's brother, Christopher stopped as the woman beside him gave a quiet sigh.

JC stuck out his hand as he approached, and Christopher took it in a firm grip while the other man sized him up. Like any protective big brother would.

It seemed Edith and Henry weren't the only ones picking up the vibes between him and his lovely companion.

"Hello, Heather." Christopher nodded at the elegant tearoom owner.

She tucked her hand in her husband's arm as she returned his greeting, a twitch of—amusement?—playing at the corners of her mouth.

"You're still welcome to join us for brunch—unless you have other plans?" JC eyed Marci.

"I thought I'd borrow Heather's computer and work on the elder-assistance plan."

His forehead puckered. "You're not supposed to work on

Sunday. This should be a day of rest and relaxation and fun. With other people."

Subtlety wasn't JC's strong suit. You'd have to be dense as a block of dried Nantucket peat to miss the blatant hint.

Marci wasn't dense.

She stepped close to her brother and tipped up her chin—as in-your-face as she could get, given the height difference. "I won't be here long, JC—and I want to make as much progress as I can on the plan. In fact, if you don't mind, you and Heather can drop me off at the house on your way to eat and save Christopher a trip."

"I don't mind taking you home." Christopher rejoined the conversation.

"Thank you—but this is more practical."

And it also sent a clear message to her brother. Back off. Butt out. Don't push.

"We'll be happy to run you home, Marci. Right, JC?" Heather nudged her husband.

He gave his sister a disgruntled scowl, clearly not pleased with the outcome of the conversation.

"Thanks, Heather." Marci repositioned herself beside her sister-in-law. "Thanks for introducing me to Reverend Kaizer, Christopher."

"My pleasure."

Marci linked her arm with her brother's, and with Heather's cooperation propelled him toward the car.

Disappointed as he was to lose another few minutes in her company, Christopher couldn't help but grin at Marci's take-charge attitude. She was one feisty woman. If her deft handling of her brother was any indication, very few people managed to outmaneuver her.

"Lovely girl, isn't she?"

He shifted around to find Edith once more approaching. "Yes, she is—with a very protective brother."

"JC feels a strong sense of responsibility for his siblings. He raised them after their mother died, you know."

"I heard part of that story."

"He just wants what's best for Marci."

"I can understand that."

"In that case, you and he will hit it off fine. Well, it's off to The Flake for sugar doughnuts. I'll talk to Marci later today and see how I can help with that plan of yours." She signaled to Chester, who was talking to another older man across the lawn, and the two met up halfway across the expanse of green.

Keys in hand, Christopher wandered toward his car, Edith's comment about JC wanting what was best for Marci replaying in his mind.

The question was, what *was* best for her?

Given how she'd ditched him for different transportation home, it was clear she didn't think it was a relationship between them.

Until a few days ago, he hadn't thought it would be in *his* best interest, either.

But perhaps there was potential they should explore.

So before too much more of her vacation slipped away, they should have a serious conversation about this subject—or an opportunity they might both live to regret would disappear into the clouds along with the jet that would carry her home.

* * *

The massive garden rehab job was finished.

Wiping her hands on her jeans, Marci stepped up onto

Henry's back porch and surveyed the yard. After nine days of hard work, the garden lining three sides of the fence was pristine. The myriad of flowers planted by Henry's wife had been freed from their weedy prison, the blending of heights and colors and textures a testament to careful planning and an eye for beauty.

Today marked another milestone too.

Her lips curved up.

Henry was leaving the hospital for the assisted-living facility—or the rehab center, as she'd taken to calling it, to reinforce the temporary nature of his stay.

But the older man still wasn't happy about it. He wanted to come home. Sooner rather than later.

On a happier note, his daughter had gone. Meaning his life was much more peaceful.

Marci gathered up the gardening tools, glancing at Christopher's cottage as she lugged them toward the storage shed. No sign of him.

Good.

Why add more fuel to the fire?

Especially with Edith and JC already peppering her with questions about their relationship—Edith taking the subtle approach, always prefaced by the delivery of a sweet treat to her cottage, while JC had been much more direct.

Both, however, had been after the same information.

Too bad.

As her peeved brother had remarked, she'd closed up tight as a Nantucket quahog—and she wasn't about to open up anytime soon.

She stowed the rake and hoe in the corner of the shed and laid her well-broken-in gardening gloves on the counter.

What was the point of discussing the subject, anyway? There was no future for her and Christopher. Besides the fact that she was only a visitor to the island, their backgrounds were too different. He was a doctor. She was an unemployed social worker. He came from wealth, vacationing with his family on pricey Nantucket every year—for *three weeks*. Her idea of vacation was an El ride to the lake with a sack lunch on a rare free Sunday afternoon.

And then there was his love for children and his support of the pro-life movement. A deal-breaker in itself.

She bolted the shed door and brushed the dirt off her hands.

Steering clear of Christopher was the sensible course, no question about it—and timing her garden work and hospital visits during his office hours had been prudent. That left her the remainder of the day to work on his plan—which thankfully was coming along well and had elicited an enthusiastic response from all the contacts she'd made. At this rate, it ought to be ready to implement before she left.

And the icing on the cake? Along the way, she'd rounded up all the resources Henry would need after he came home to his cottage.

She paused near the side of the house and gave the garden a final sweep.

It was beautiful. Renewed and refreshed, ready to thrive now that all the noxious elements had been removed.

If only she could do the same with her soul.

But as she walked through the rose arbor, even the sweet-scented air couldn't vanquish the sudden melancholy that dampened her spirits.

10

On Thursday afternoon, Marci rounded the corner in the hall at the rehab center—and came face-to-face with Christopher.

As she stumbled back in surprise, his hand shot out to steady her. "Sorry."

In the second it took her to regain her balance, the timing of his visit registered. His presence here in the middle of office hours didn't bode well.

"Is Henry okay?"

"He's running a slight temperature. There's a bit of inflammation around the incision, which could be the cause. But with his compromised immune system, we're being aggressive with antibiotics."

"It must be serious or you wouldn't have interrupted office hours."

"I had a no-show. That gave me a window to run over. I think he'll be fine, but we'll be keeping close watch over him."

"Is he up to a visitor?"

Humor glinted in his cobalt irises. "If her name is Patricia, no. If her name is Marci, yes. I had to promise not to tell his daughter about this glitch, by the way."

"I can understand that."

"Me too." He twisted his wrist and scanned his watch. "I

have to run. Go on in. Your visit will cheer him up. His spirits could use a boost today."

"One boost coming right up." She handed him the file that she'd tucked under her arm. "I was going to leave this with Henry and ask him to pass it on to you. It's a semifinal draft of your plan. Before I go any further, I wanted to get your reaction. See you later."

As she continued down the hall, the urge to peek back and see if Christopher was watching her was strong.

But she could resist until she got to Henry's room, three doors down.

She made it—barely.

Yet once she crossed the threshold, all thoughts of the distracting doctor vanished.

Since her visit yesterday, Henry seemed to have aged ten years. He was lying down rather than sitting up as he had been when they'd chatted less than twenty-four hours ago, and his cheeks were sunken and flushed.

Yet when his eyelids flickered open, he managed a weary smile. "Hello, Marci. Come to visit an old man, I see."

Somehow she coaxed up the corners of her lips. "No. I came to visit one of the most youthful men I know."

"In spirit, maybe. Too bad the body can't keep up."

Bad attitude. It held a disturbing hint of surrender.

"I saw Christopher in the hallway." She drew up a chair beside the bed. "He told me you have a slight temperature, but he didn't seem too concerned. As far as I know, you're on track to ditch this place sometime next week."

He brushed his gnarled fingers over the sheet that covered him. "Maybe."

"Henry Calhoun!" Marci took his hand in a firm grip. "After

all the work I've done to put a whole army of resources at your disposal, I expect you to march out this door next week. Meals-on-wheels, a personal shopper, rides to medical appointments, pharmacy deliveries...you name it. Besides, I'm missing your banana-nut bread."

His mouth flexed. "I'm kind of missing that myself." He patted her hand. "We'll see. Let's take it a day at a time."

He was giving up. Marci could hear it his voice. See it in his resigned expression. Feel it in his consoling pat of her hand.

"Henry." She leaned closer, posture taut. "You *are* going to go home. You can't let Patricia win."

He squinted at her. "That *would* be a shame, wouldn't it?"

"You bet. You have a lot of good years left—at home, in your cottage. I finished the garden, by the way. I can't wait for you to see it. In fact, why don't we plan a picnic dinner out there your first night back?"

"I'd like that."

She stood and leaned down to press a kiss to his too-warm forehead. "We have a date, then—and I don't like being stood up. Can I count on you to be there?"

A touch of his old spark flared to life. "I'll do my best."

"Good. I'll be back later tonight. Why don't I bring you one of those chocolate tarts you liked at tea?"

"They sure were tasty."

"Done. I'll raid Heather's kitchen. Try to rest this afternoon."

"Not much else I can do. Take care, Marci."

She crossed to the door, blew him a kiss, and retraced her steps down the hall. While the facility was well-kept, and colorful Fourth of July decorations brightened the common rooms in anticipation of the coming holiday, an oppressive sense of gloom hung over the place. The hallway was filled with residents hunched in wheelchairs or shuffling along behind walkers.

Could there be a more depressing place to live?

Christopher was right. Henry would wither and die here. They had to get him out as soon as possible.

And in the meantime, she had to give him an incentive to keep fighting.

But where could she turn for inspiration?

Ask, and you shall receive.

Her step faltered.

Where had *that* come from?

The source clicked into place. Reverend Kaizer had read those words last Sunday. They were from the Bible. A promise from God.

She started forward again, more slowly. Could this be one of the situations where prayer would make a difference? It had done the trick with Nathan last year, when she and JC had visited him in his darkest hour.

What did she have to lose?

As she stepped into the sunlight, Marci stopped, drew a deep, cleansing breath of the fresh Nantucket air, and sent a silent plea toward the heavens.

God, I have no idea if you're listening. I kind of doubt it, since we haven't exactly been on speaking terms. But if you are, could you help my friend, Henry? He's a good man, and I don't think he's ready to check out yet. But he needs encouragement. Please lift his spirits—and help me think of something that will make him realize how much he's loved and how much we want him to get better.

There. It was done.

Now all she could do was hope for a response.

***

Wow.

Christopher flipped over the last page of the plan Marci had put together and took a sip of his cooling coffee.

She'd done a fabulous job weaving a bunch of random ideas into a coherent proposal. Her plan relied on contributions from area residents, businesses, churches, and organizations, and she'd already lined up an impressive level of funding commitments and support. Plus, she'd compiled a comprehensive database of volunteers willing to assist with the effort or participate in the time bank. And the high-school administration had embraced the notion of youth involvement and promised to promote it.

The plan was also very professional—well-organized, well-thought-out, and well-presented. The rationale was compelling, the payback to the community clearly outlined.

He rose from the kitchen table in his cottage and rinsed his mug in the sink.

There was only one recommendation he'd change in Marci's proposal. She'd suggested the organization be run by a volunteer committee. But in light of the scale and complexity of the coordination required for optimal function, a more formalized structure—and an office—were warranted.

The office shouldn't be difficult to arrange. Months ago, when he'd mentioned the idea to a few people at the hospital, word had spread to top management—and one of the executives had indicated a willingness to donate office space.

That deserved a follow-up first thing tomorrow.

As for structure—Marci's program deserved a full-time, professional director. It should be run by someone with credentials in social service work and an affinity for the elderly.

MEANT FOR EACH OTHER

Someone like Marci.

Would she be willing to stay on and take the job?

More importantly, should he *ask* her to stay?

Mulling that over, he pushed through the back door into the deepening twilight and ambled across the lawn to survey Henry's garden over the picket fence.

Order had been restored, and the plants and flowers were once more reaching for the sky, free to bloom now that they'd been liberated from the choking weeds that had blocked them from the sun and sucked the life from them.

Henry would be pleased.

And if he were standing here now, odds were his neighbor would be drawing an analogy. Telling him to free himself from the restraints of his past that kept love from taking root. To lift his face to the sun and give his heart new life.

With Marci.

As if on cue, she appeared from around the far side of Henry's cottage, picked up the nozzle on the coiled hose behind the house, and turned on the water. Only after she swung toward the garden did she notice him.

"Oh. I didn't see you there."

"I just came out." He swept a hand over the garden. "I thought you were done here."

"I am—but I uprooted a few plants the other day while I was weeding the last patch, and I thought they could use a drink."

"You drove out from town just for that?"

She shrugged and moved toward the back of the garden, pulling the hose behind her. "After all my hard work, I don't want any casualties." She adjusted the nozzle to a soft spray and sprinkled a patch of slightly wilted flowers. "I'm glad I ran into you, though. I visited Henry again. You were right earlier today. He's down in the dumps. Even the chocolate tarts I brought him didn't cheer him up much."

"I know. I stopped in after office hours. I tried to convince him his fever is nothing more than a small detour, but I don't think I got through. I'm not sure what to try next. A positive attitude would go a long way toward helping him recover."

"I agree—and I had an idea I wanted to bounce off you. It's ambitious, though."

"So was the elder-assistance plan, but you managed to pull that off. I just read it. You did a stellar job. And I love the name you came up with. Caring Connections says it all."

She dismissed her efforts with a wave. "Thanks. But you did the hard concept part. All it needed was legwork to flesh it out."

"Nope. Don't buy it. You took a bunch of stream-of-consciousness ideas and molded them into a cohesive, workable plan. And you went out and drummed up support for it. That required talent—and a massive amount of effort. So I suspect whatever idea you've come up with to boost Henry's spirits is manageable. Tell me about it."

She moved back to the faucet, shut off the water, and began recoiling the hose. "Well, when we first met, Henry told me about the gazebo that used to be over there." She pointed to the bare spot that was rimmed by hydrangea bushes about to burst into bloom. "He said he'd built it for his wife years ago, but it had been destroyed in a storm. I got the impression it meant a lot to him."

"It did. It was his wife's favorite place. I was with him the night the storm ripped it apart. He told me that was the only spot where he could still feel her presence."

"So let's rebuild it. I saw a picture of it in Henry's kitchen, and the design doesn't seem too complicated. Chester's handy, and I bet I could get him to draw up plans. I'm sure he'd also help with the construction. And I know I could convince JC to pitch in too. With Henry scheduled to come home next week, it'll be tight—but they used to build barns in one day years ago. We could also start dropping hints to get him excited about the surprise." She kept her distance as she finished. "What do you think?"

A slow smile tugged on his lips as he envisioned the gazebo that could fill the empty space on the lawn—and in the older man's heart. "I think it's brilliant. Henry will love it."

She edged closer, until only a few feet separated them. Close enough for him to feel her almost tangible excitement. "The main problem is cost. It won't be cheap."

"Don't worry about the expense. I owe Henry a debt I can never repay. Put me down for the building crew too. I'm not the world's best carpenter, but if someone points me to a nail I can drive it in."

Her eyes began to sparkle. "Can you imagine his face when we bring him home and he sees it?"

"It will be an unforgettable moment. I have a key to Henry's house. Do you want to take the picture with you and get Chester's opinion?"

"Yes. Thanks."

"Give me a sec." He strode toward his cottage, retrieved the key, and joined her at Henry's back door. After removing the photo from the wall, he rejoined her on Henry's porch and handed it over.

While he relocked the door, she examined the image. "I would have liked to meet Marjorie."

At her soft comment, Christopher pocketed the key and scanned the picture over her shoulder. "Me too—but Henry's told me about her. They shared an amazing love. The once-in-a-lifetime kind everyone hopes to find."

She transferred her attention to him, and at the almost palpable yearning in her eyes the breath whooshed from his lungs.

Her subliminal message was clear.

She wanted him to kiss her.

But she wasn't ready for that.

He wasn't ready for that.

So instead, he pulled her into a hug, the photo of Henry's gazebo—a symbol of enduring love—captured between them.

Quivers rippled through her, but she didn't pull away. And as the seconds ticked by in the quiet of Henry's garden that was broken only by the distant crash of the surf, the tension slowly melted from her body as he rested his cheek against her curls

At last, with a shuddering breath, she eased back. Fingering the photo, she spoke in a tone that tried a little too hard to sound light and casual. "Henry's picture seems to have cast quite a spell. Pretty soon it'll have us believing in fairy tales."

Christopher locked gazes with her. "The picture isn't the only thing casting a spell—and not all romance is confined to fairy tales."

Tears welled in her eyes—along with an emotion that looked a lot like regret. "It is for me."

Before he could process that comment, she backed down the porch steps. "I have t-to go. I'll let you know what Chester says about the gazebo."

With that, she took off at a half run around the side of the cottage.

"Marci, wait." He started after her—but halted at the panicked look she threw over her shoulder when he reached the arbor.

She was telling him she needed space.

So he remained under the cascade of roses, gripping the top of the gate while she slid into her car and sped away with a churn of gravel.

Sixty seconds later, he pried his fingers off the gate, took a deep breath, and returned to the yard—pausing to survey the spot that had once held the gazebo built with loving care by Henry for a woman whose love continued to enrich his life.

That was what he wanted. The kind of love shared by Henry and Marjorie—and by his own parents. Yes, he'd made an error in judgment once, mistaking neediness for love. And a deep-seated wariness was a lasting souvenir of the tragic consequences of that relationship.

But Marci wasn't Denise. Of that he was certain.

Yet given her comment tonight about fairy tales—and her hasty exit when the atmosphere began to get romantic—she did have issues. And they *could* be as scary as Denise's.

So before she boarded a plane for Chicago in two short weeks, he had to find out what they were.

Because if he let her walk away, the brightness she'd added to his days would fade away as quickly as clouds could snuff out the Nantucket sun.

11

"I can't believe how fast this came together."

At Marci's comment, Christopher took a long pull on his lemonade and surveyed the gazebo that had risen in Henry's backyard in the course of one Sunday afternoon, a mere three days after she'd broached the idea. "Me, neither. Another half hour ought to wrap it up. We couldn't have done it without Chester, though." He lifted his cup toward the older man in overalls who was perched on a ladder securing a decorative piece of lattice while JC held it in place and Edith directed the process from ground level.

"When I gave him the photo, he rubbed his hands together and said, 'I love projects.' Edith warned me he tends to be slow—she said it took him more than two years to restore the cottage I'm staying in—but she must have lit a fire under him. He came out here Friday afternoon, drew the plans up that night, and bought all the materials yesterday. It's amazing. And I think our little scheme is working. When I dropped a few hints to Henry about a surprise, I could tell his interest was piqued." Excitement put a becoming flush on her cheeks.

Man, he'd missed her since she'd been keeping herself scarce after that hug on Henry's porch.

"It is. He's been trying to finagle information out of me whenever I visit."

"More to the right, Chester." Edith's voice rang across the yard. "The lattice is sticking out on the other side over the opening."

"She'd make a first-rate foreman." Christopher hitched up one side of his mouth and walked a few feet away to pick up another piece of trim. "You want to help me put this up?"

"Sure."

He set his disposable cup aside and moved back to the gazebo. After positioning a ladder beside the opening next to Chester, he took the lattice from Marci.

"I'm sorry to run out on you, but we have plans for tonight." Edith steadied the adjacent ladder as her husband descended. "You and Marci can handle the last two pieces of trim, can't you?"

"We don't have to rush, Edith." The older man stepped off the ladder.

"Chester." She elbowed him. "We have to leave. *Now.*"

Squinting at her, he took off his baseball cap and scratched his head, leaving his unruly cowlick in disarray. "I guess we do."

Edith turned to JC. "Didn't Heather ask you to be back by seven? You could hitch a ride home with us and leave the car for Marci to use later."

He looked from his neighbor to his sister and hoisted up one side of his mouth. "Sounds like a plan."

Christopher propped one shoulder against the gazebo and watched the show. Edith's masterful maneuvering was impressive.

But it was clear from Marci's mutinous expression that she didn't share his reaction. "None of you said anything earlier about having to leave at a certain time."

"I assumed we'd be done by now. But that's what happens

when you have an amateur crew." Edith began to bustle about, collecting the scraps of wood while Chester and JC broke down the portable sawhorses and loaded them into Chester's truck. "You want us to leave one of the ladders, Christopher?"

"If you don't mind. I can use Henry's, but it would help if Marci had one too so she can balance the trim in place while I attach it."

"No problem. Chester gets out this way at least once a week. He'll pick it up on his next trip." Edith planted her hands on her ample hips and surveyed the gazebo. "A mighty fine job. I imagine Henry will be pleased."

Christopher checked on Marci. Her arms were folded tightly across her chest, and she was frowning.

Not promising. If she stayed behind under duress, it would be awkward.

"Would you rather leave with your brother?" Christopher dropped his volume.

She bit her lower lip. "Can you finish this alone?"

"It would be easier with another pair of hands. Besides, I have a few things I wanted to discuss with you about Caring Connections."

She shot the cleanup trio another glance. Huffed out a breath. "Look—in case you haven't realized it, Edith has a penchant for matchmaking."

His lips quirked. "Yeah. I figured that out."

"I don't want to encourage her—or my brother. It makes no sense for a host of reasons, not the least of which is my imminent departure."

"I'd like to talk to you about that too."

Before she could respond, Edith called out to them. "We're off. Be sure to get that trim on straight, Christopher."

"I will. Thanks for all your help. You too, Chester and JC."

There were a flurry of goodbyes, followed by the cough of a truck engine as it turned over and the crunch of tires on oyster shells. Then silence descended, save for the rhythmic pounding of the surf.

Given Marci's silence, she must still be processing his last comment. A discussion about her departure hadn't been in his plans for today—but if she intended to continue avoiding him, it could be his best opportunity to put out feelers about her interest in the director job.

And in him.

Trim in hand, he climbed the ladder. "Let's finish this up before we lose the light."

Without a word, Marci ascended the other ladder, grasped the trim, and held it in place while Christopher secured it.

For the next fifteen minutes, their communication was confined to mechanics—"A little more to the right...raise it an inch on your side...straighten it a bit." She didn't ask him to explain his comment. He didn't offer to.

After the last screw was seated in the wood, Christopher put Henry's ladder in the toolshed and leaned Chester's against the railing of the back porch. Then he joined Marci, who had moved off to examine the gazebo from across the yard.

The step-up structure was simple in design, the only ornamentation the lattice panels above each opening and a picketed railing. Constructed of natural wood, it had the hue of fresh-cut lumber. But it wouldn't take long for the gazebo to acquire the driftwood-colored patina of its predecessor. Large enough to accommodate a café table or a pair of wicker rocking chairs, it would be a wonderful place for Henry to recuperate—and remember.

"I can picture Henry sitting there with a mug of coffee in his hand, can't you?" She tucked one of her wayward curls behind her ear.

"You're reading my mind."

"What's your best guess on when he might come home?"

"He didn't have a fever this morning when I stopped by. That's a positive sign. If he continues to progress, I'd say he could be back here by Thursday."

"That would be ideal. It would give me a chance to be certain all the help I lined up is working out before I leave."

A tailor-made opening.

He motioned toward the gazebo. "Why don't we sit for a minute? May as well enjoy the fruits of our labors."

After a brief hesitation, she crossed the lawn and sat on the elevated floor at the entrance, as close as possible to the upright post on one side.

He joined her in the ample space she'd left for him. After stretching out his legs, he crossed his ankles and leaned back on his palms. The lush green grass and colorful, well-tended flower beds inside the picket fence provided a striking contrast to the golden sand and sparkling sea beyond. "Henry has a beautiful spot here."

"Too bad Patricia can't appreciate that. And how much it means to him." She clasped her hands around one knee. "You know, after visiting him at that assisted-living facility, I can't imagine anyone wanting to end their days in a place like that. I'm glad your plan will give older folks another option."

"At this point, it's your plan as much as it is mine."

"No, it was your idea. But I'm glad I could help give it life."

This was the moment to broach his idea.

Christopher took a steadying breath. "I'd like for you to do more than that."

Twin furrows appeared on her brow. "What do you mean?"

"You saw my note about the program deserving a full-time director?"

"Yes."

"With your social-work degree, organizational skills, and empathy for the elderly, you have all the credentials for the job."

Several beats of silence ticked by. "You mean until you find a permanent director?"

"No. I think you'd be an excellent permanent director."

"I'd have to move here."

"I know—and I can appreciate what that means. You'd have to disrupt your whole life in Chicago. Leave behind everything you know. But you may have to relocate for a new job anyway, and your brother lives here, so it wouldn't be as if—"

His phone began to vibrate, and he stifled a groan. Could the timing be any worse?

Tempted as he was to ignore it, years of medical training had hardwired him to respond to every call.

He pulled the phone off his belt and skimmed the screen. "It's my exchange. I have to take this."

"Go ahead."

He pressed the talk button. "Christopher Morgan. Hold a moment, please." Tapping mute, he stood. "I'll tell you what. Why don't we grab sandwiches in town and talk about this? It's past dinnertime. Think about it while I deal with this."

Without waiting for her to respond, he moved across the yard.

Praying she wouldn't think up an excuse to cut their evening short—or refuse the job outright.

* * *

Thank goodness the call from Christopher's exchange had bought her a few minutes to think.

From her perch on the edge of Henry's gazebo, Marci scanned the far horizon where sea met sky. The vista that had once beckoned Nantucket whalers.

As this job beckoned her.

It was a superb fit.

As she'd discovered over the past few weeks, she had an affinity for older folks—and helping people like Henry retain their independence would be satisfying, rewarding work.

As for Christopher's concern about her giving up her life in Chicago? Her lips twisted. That would be no sacrifice. Her fond memories of the Windy City would fit in a thimble.

But this job offer wasn't only about Caring Connections.

It was also about *personal* connections.

He wanted her to stay because he thought the sparks between them could also lead to something permanent.

If only.

Throat tightening, she watched him as he spoke on the phone, brow furrowed, his full attention on whatever patient required his help. Giving his all—as he always did. This kind, caring, compassionate man reeked of integrity.

Bottom line, Christopher Morgan was the real deal.

But understanding as he was, would he be able to overlook her past?

Unknown.

And that was a hurdle they'd have to clear before she agreed to stay—*after* she had a chance to work up her courage to tell him her story.

Christopher slipped his phone back onto his belt and rejoined her. "What's the word on dinner? The 'Sconset Café has great sandwiches. We could pick up a couple and enjoy them on the beach while we talk."

"I need to think about your suggestion, Christopher."

"Understood. But you also have to eat. At least join me for a bite. We deserve it after all our hard work this afternoon. And I promise not to push about the job. Tonight, anyway."

She hesitated. Dinner on the beach with the handsome man smiling down at her sounded like heaven, but what if—

"Don't overthink it, Marci. It's just sandwiches."

Go for it, girl. You may never have this chance again.

That was true. And what harm could there be in a casual dinner? "Sold."

"Great. Let me get a beach towel from the house."

Sixty seconds later, they were strolling down the narrow lane toward the center of the tiny village. Honoring his promise, he didn't bring up the job again. Instead, he kept the conversation light. Once they arrived at the small restaurant, already packed for the evening meal, they worked their way through the crowd and placed their order with a hostess who greeted him by name. A teen behind the counter also offered a friendly wave.

"You must be a regular." Marci squeezed through the throng of customers as he ushered her back toward the deck in front.

"I come here three or four nights a week. Everyone knows me." He pushed the door open and they stepped outside to wait for their order to be called. "That's not unusual in a town the size of 'Sconset. It doesn't take long to distinguish the year-rounders from the day-trippers and summer people—and ninety-eight percent of the people here during the summer fall into the latter two categories." He scanned the diners enjoying their meal at tables on the large deck. "I don't recognize any—"

When he stopped speaking, Marci looked up at him. His

complexion had lost several shades of color, and his features were taut.

What in the world?

She turned to follow the direction of his gaze. A woman in her late fifties or early sixties, seated at a table for two on the other side of the deck, was staring at him. As Marci watched, she spoke to her gray-haired companion. He shifted toward them, and the icy glare he aimed at Christopher sent a shiver down her spine, despite the balmy weather.

"What's wrong, Christopher?"

Instead of answering, he took her arm and guided her back inside. "Let's see if our food is ready."

He left her by the door, strode to the counter, and spoke to the hostess. She disappeared into the kitchen, and rather than rejoin her as he waited, Christopher remained where he was. Although Marci couldn't see his face, the tense line of his broad shoulders and his stiff stance communicated distress with a capital D.

What was going on?

A couple of minutes later, the hostess reappeared with two packages wrapped in white paper. She slid them into a large bag, added cans of soda and cellophane-wrapped utensils, and handed the bag to Christopher.

When he turned back, his features had shifted into neutral. "Let's find a spot on the beach." Avoiding eye contact with the two people who'd lasered venom his direction, he took her arm and led her across the elevated wooden platform.

But Marci checked on them as they left.

They were still watching Christopher, their hate so palpable it sent a jolt ricocheting through her.

Why would anyone hate such a kind, caring, decent man?

Christopher didn't offer any explanation. Nor did he speak again until they reached the sand.

"Why don't we go down there and avoid the crowd?" He swept a hand to the right, where deserted beach stretched before them.

"Fine by me."

They trudged through the deep sand in silence. After about fifty yards he stopped, unrolled the towel he'd tucked under his arm, and spread it out. They both sat, and he retrieved the sodas from the bag. But when he tried to open one of the cans, he couldn't get his trembling fingers to cooperate.

Her stomach clenched.

Whatever had rattled him was bad. Very bad.

She leaned over and took the can from him, gentling her voice. "Let me."

After popping the tab, she handed it back and opened the other one for herself.

When he reached into the bag for their sandwiches, she laid a hand on his arm. "Let's sit for a few minutes. I have a feeling you're not in the mood to eat just now."

Nor was she. Her stomach was churning.

He took a long swallow of his soda. "Sorry. I never expected to see those people again. It was a bit of a jolt."

"I could tell." She ran a finger around the rim of her can, a proceed-with-caution warning flashing in her mind. A woman who had secrets of her own had no business butting into anyone else's private territory. "Do you want to tell me who they are?"

He took a deep breath and focused on the sea. The shadows were deepening as the day wound down, robbing the blue water of its sparkle. "They were part of a very dark chapter in my life. The chapter that led me to Nantucket."

She sifted sand through her fingers. "I wondered why you

came here." She chose her words with care. "I asked Henry a few discreet questions, but the most I ever got out of him was that you needed a change. I suspected there was more to the story."

"There is. I hadn't planned to get into it tonight—but there has to be a reason for God's timing on this. There always is." He raked his fingers through his hair. "It's not what I'd call dinner conversation, though. And it's not pretty."

"We can put off dinner for a while."

Twin furrows appeared on his brow as he swirled his soda.

Marci remained silent. If he wanted to share the story, fine. If he didn't—she wouldn't push.

At last he set his soda in the sand beside him, rested his forearms on his knees, and fixed his attention on the horizon. "Those people are the parents of a woman I dated in Boston. Her name was Denise. I met her at a charity event when she lost her footing going down a step and sprained her ankle. I did a quick exam and suggested she have it X-rayed. She was there with a girlfriend who offered to drive her to the ER, so I helped her out to the car and wished her well." He turned toward her, his face haggard. "Have you ever had a moment in your life that, in hindsight, you knew was a turning point? One where, if you could relive it, you'd make a different decision?"

Her stomach knotted, and she forced air into her lungs. "Yes."

"That's what that night was like for me. If I had it to do over again, I would never have stepped forward to help."

"That would have been out of character for you."

"Maybe. But my life after that would have been far less traumatic—and I wouldn't be so cautious around women in distress...or freaked out by tears."

Marci studied him. "I've gotten teary-eyed around you, and

I haven't noticed you freaking out."

"I did the first night, when I saw you crying in the restaurant. But after I got to know you, I realized that tears aren't your standard operating procedure."

"They were with Denise?"

"Not at first." He picked up his soda and took a long drink. "She was grateful for my help at the party, and the next day a huge cookie bouquet arrived at my office. I thought it was overkill, but sweet. Two days later she called and invited me to a symphony concert. We had an enjoyable evening, and I reciprocated with an invitation to a movie. Over the next month we went out quite a bit."

He stopped—and when the silence lengthened, Marci spoke. "It sounds like a normal dating relationship."

"It didn't stay normal." His fingers flexed on the soda can, denting the side, and he set it back on the sand. "She became very possessive. Started calling me three or four times a day. I began to feel smothered. So one night at dinner I told her I thought we should give each other more space, move more slowly."

"She didn't respond well?"

"No. She started crying, pleading with me not to reject her, saying she'd do anything as long as I promised to keep seeing her. She was creating such a scene that we left the restaurant before they served our entrées. I tried to reason with her in the car on the way home, but I couldn't get through. Her reaction was over the top. That's when I realized she had serious psychological issues."

"That's a tough situation to be in." More so for a man with a compassionate heart who devoted his life to relieving pain, not creating it.

"Yeah." He wiped a hand down his face. "After that night, I

knew there was no future in the relationship. But she wouldn't accept that. The phone calls increased, and she'd leave hysterical messages on my answering machine. She began sending me expensive gifts. When I stopped responding, she started showing up at my condo. Just hanging around, waiting for me to come home from work."

Marci suppressed a shiver. "That's scary."

"Tell me about it. I had no idea how to deal with that kind of obsessiveness. I finally told her I was going to call the police unless she left me alone."

"What happened then?"

He stared at the darkening sea. "She threatened to commit suicide if I cut her off."

Marci drew in a sharp breath. "That's emotional blackmail."

"I know." He massaged the bridge of his nose. "I'd met her parents. We'd had brunch at their house once. So I called to express my concern. They laid into me too, accusing me of leading her on. And they refused to acknowledge she had any problems. It was a mess."

That term didn't begin to capture his obvious anguish and pain.

"Did you see her again?"

"Once. I met her at the Public Garden on my lunch hour one day. She worked near there as a receptionist at a real-estate office her father owned. I only did it because she sounded desperate, and I hoped I could convince her to seek professional help. But it was a mistake. She had another meltdown." He picked up his can of soda, took another long drink, then crushed the fragile aluminum in his hand. "The next day she took her life by swallowing a lethal combination of pills."

As the shocking revelation sank in, Marci's stomach twisted into a hard knot. "Oh, Christopher. I'm so sorry."

"So was I." His voice roughened, and he cleared his throat. "The guilt was crushing. I felt her death was my fault, and that there must have been something I could have done."

"What?"

"I don't know. But her parents certainly thought I was to blame, based on the letter they sent me. She was their only child."

"Why couldn't they see she needed help?"

"I can't answer that. Maybe it's easier to pretend a problem doesn't exist than to do the hard work of addressing it in a responsible way."

That was true. She'd walked that road—with the same tragic results.

When she didn't respond, Christopher turned to her. "This was more than you wanted to know, wasn't it?"

"No." She forced her own regrets aside to focus on him. "I'm honored you shared the story with me—and I'm sorrier than I can say for all the pain it's caused you. I assume that's what prompted you to give up your practice and move here?"

"Yes. I started over—but continued to struggle with the guilt."

"It wasn't your fault, Christopher."

"I'm beginning to believe that. But it *has* made me question my judgment about women. However…I'm regaining my confidence on that score too—thanks to you."

Or not.

She didn't have Denise's psychological issues, but she did have secrets—and once he learned them, they could be as big a turnoff as the problems of his Boston girlfriend.

Time to change the tenor of this conversation.

She picked up her soda and lightened her tone. "Well, *I'm* confident we'll be eating in the dark if we don't dig into our sandwiches. Are you in the mood for dinner, or should we call it a night?"

"I can eat. To be honest, it felt freeing to talk about what happened. The only other person here who's heard my story is Henry." He reached into the bag and withdrew the sandwiches. After handing hers over, he began to unwrap his.

"What did he have to say about it?" Marci peeled back the paper on the sandwich she didn't want.

"Same as you. That what happened with Denise wasn't my fault. That the problem was hers, not mine. Henry is very loyal."

"And right."

"It took me a long while to accept that—but after a lot of prayer and reflection, I'm finally coming around." He took a bite of his sandwich.

Marci followed his lead, forcing herself to chew and swallow. "Speaking of Henry—why don't we talk about his coming-home party?"

"Good idea. I'm ready for a happier topic."

For the rest of their meal, they focused on the older man. And by the time they walked back down the oystershell lane toward his cottage, the tension in Marci's shoulders had relaxed.

"Thanks for dinner." She dug through her purse for her key as they stopped beside her car

"It was my pleasure." He leaned against the hood and folded his arms over his chest, obviously in no hurry to end the evening.

And what a gorgeous evening it was. A full moon overhead gave an ethereal glow to the landscape, and a glimpse of the shimmering sea between Henry's cottage and the one Christopher occupied was visible.

It could have been the setting for a romantic scene in a movie.

But this was real-life, not a Hollywood fantasy.

Quashing her whimsical thoughts, she tossed her purse onto the passenger seat. "I'll see you soon."

He pushed off from the hood and moved closer.

Too close.

"I have something I want to ask you. Not related to the job."

Heart racing, she gripped the edge of the door with one hand as he stopped in front of her. "Okay."

"My parents are coming to Nantucket for a couple of days this week. We're planning to go to dinner on Tuesday. I'd be honored if you'd join us."

He was inviting her to meet his parents.

Wow.

"I...uh...wouldn't want them to get the wrong idea—if you know what I mean."

"I know what you mean." He reached up and traced the curve of her jaw with a gentle finger. "And I think they'll get exactly the right idea."

Her breath hitched. "This isn't...smart."

"I disagree." His fingers brushed her lips, sending liquid fire through her veins. "We've been dancing around the attraction between us since the beginning, Marci. I think we need to explore it. Don't you?"

She'd answer—if she could form a coherent sentence. But with Christopher a whisper away and the moon silvering the world around her, she couldn't seem to engage the left side of her brain.

One side of his mouth hitched up. "I don't think I've ever rendered a woman speechless before—but I do agree that talk is superfluous."

Resting one hand lightly on her shoulder, he captured one of her springy curls in his strong, lean fingers. Then, eyes darkening, he kissed her.

Marci stopped breathing.

Oh, mercy.

It had been years since she'd been kissed. And never like this. With tenderness…and reverence….and deep respect and caring.

If it lasted forever, the kiss would be too short.

Unfortunately, Christopher backed off far too soon, leaving her still clinging to the door—and to his shirt.

Whoops.

She'd bunched the front into her fist, and she forced herself to release the handful of wrinkles.

"Did I convince you to have dinner with us?" His voice had deepened, and a delicious tingle raced through her.

"Yes." What else could she say after that mind-blowing kiss?

His smile warmed her all the way to her toes. "I'll call you with the details." After a moment, he backed off. "Drive safe."

She nodded, not trusting her voice.

It took her two tries to get the key into the ignition. And as she pulled away, her gaze flitted between the road and her rearview mirror, where the tall, broad-shouldered man bathed in moonlight was reflected.

He was like a figure from a dream. The sort of man a lonely woman would conjure up in her imagination to fill the empty place in her heart.

Except Christopher Morgan was real.

But when moonlight and dreams gave way to reality and the harsh light of day, would he continue to hang around—or would he vanish like the mist of a Nantucket morning?

12

"I'm perfectly capable of doing that myself, thank you."

As Henry shooed away the aide who was trying to help him put on his robe, Marci paused in the doorway. On each of her visits to the assisted-living facility in the past few days, he'd been livelier.

Spotting her, he grinned. "My favorite visitor."

"If you need me, ring the bell, Mr. Calhoun." The young aide skirted around him.

"I'll do that. But I expect I'll be fine. Especially now that I have such a pretty lady to chat with."

As the woman exited, Marci strolled over to Henry. "You're looking good."

"I'm feeling much improved—and getting awful tired of this place."

"Christopher says he expects to spring you on Thursday—just in time for Independence Day. How appropriate is that?"

"Couldn't be better." He motioned her to a chair near the window and took the facing one. "He was in this morning. Mentioned you were having dinner with him and his parents tonight."

She shifted in her seat. "He caught me at a weak moment."

"Don't you like him?"

"Sure. What's not to like?" She tried for a flippant tone. "But I don't want to give his parents the wrong impression."

"What impression would that be?"

"You know—that we're...involved."

Henry leaned back and smirked at her. "'There are none so blind as those who will not see,' to quote a very old saying. It's still true today too."

Marci narrowed her eyes. "What's that supposed to mean?"

"I may be up in years, but there's nothing wrong with my powers of perception. Anyone in the same room with you two would have to be dead not to pick up on the chemistry."

Give it up, Marci. You can't fool Henry.

With a sigh of capitulation, she slumped back in her chair. "I'll concede there may be a spark."

"A spark?" Henry hooted. "My dear girl, it's like Fourth of July."

She made a face. "Very funny. However, that still doesn't mean there's anything going on."

"There *should* be."

"Why are you so interested anyway?"

"Because I've been after that boy for two years to find himself a woman to romance. Not just any woman, mind you. Someone good and kind and smart and funny and spunky. I knew the minute we met that you two were meant for each other. And you know it too."

Geez.

Was she *that* transparent about her feelings?

But while she might *wish* that was true, she could never be worthy of a man like Christopher, no matter how much JC tried to build up her self-esteem. Her only hope was that Christopher could find a way to reconcile himself to her past.

But the odds weren't in her favor.

And if a man with such a kind and generous heart wasn't able to make peace with it, there wasn't a man alive who could.

Shoving that depressing thought aside, she wagged a finger at the older man. "Don't read too much into this dinner with Christopher's parents, Henry. He and I have never even been out on a date."

"I bet he's kissed you, though."

Hard as she tried, she couldn't stop the sudden rush of heat that flooded her cheeks.

"Hot dog!" Henry slapped his hand against his thigh, grinning ear to ear. "I'm proud of that boy. I always knew he had outstanding judgment, and this proves it." He cocked his head. "I'm guessing he told you about Denise."

"Yes—and it's also clear he wants to be cautious." A few gray clouds scuttled across the blue expanse outside the window. "The truth is, I may not be the best woman for him, Henry. There are a ton of factors working against us."

"Name one."

"We come from very different worlds in terms of family life, finances, and culture."

"Name an important one."

"That *is* important."

"No, it's not. If Marjorie and I could find a way to make it work, you can too."

She squinted at him. "What do you mean?"

"Marjorie and I met at a USO dance. Prettiest gal I'd ever seen. She had a first-class brain too. My kind of woman. We both felt the spark right away."

"Love at first sight?"

"More or less. Trouble was, her father was a self-made man with a fifth-grade education who didn't much value formal schooling. He'd risen to the top in his field and amassed a fortune after learning everything he needed to know in the school of hard knocks. By his standards, he was successful. He'd built a flourishing company, had an impressive house in a toney neighborhood, didn't want for any material possession. And he was determined that the man who married his daughter would measure up to that yardstick."

"That wasn't you?"

"Not by a long shot. My idea of success was opening the minds of young people to the works of Shakespeare, or helping them learn to appreciate and love the masterful use of language."

When he stopped, Marci leaned forward. "How did you reconcile that difference?"

"We didn't. But that didn't stop Marjorie from loving me. She said she didn't care about all the trappings of wealth. That none of that mattered if she couldn't have the man she loved. So she left it all behind. And I don't think she ever regretted it, not for one second. We had a wonderful life together here on Nantucket."

Marci's heart melted. "That's a beautiful story, Henry."

"True too. And if it worked out for me, it can work out for you."

If the only stumbling block with Christopher was their different backgrounds, Henry might be right. He didn't strike her as the type of man who would let differences in class or financial status dictate his circle of acquaintances—or choice of wife.

But there was much more they'd have to overcome.

"You don't seem convinced."

At the older man's comment, she refocused on him. "I'm supposed to leave in less than two weeks."

"Christopher told me he offered you the director job for Caring Connections."

She played with the zipper on her purse. "I haven't decided what to do about that."

"You want my opinion? Take it. You can always go back to Chicago if the pieces here don't fall into place. One lesson I've learned in life is never pass up an opportunity. Some of them only come around once." He let a few beats pass, then leaned forward with an impish grin. "Now give me another hint about this surprise you and Christopher have cooked up for me at home."

Forcing herself to switch gears, Marci bantered back and forth with the older man, evading his questions about the surprise while dropping a few more tantalizing hints.

Half an hour later, when Henry pushed her out the door to go get ready for her date—as he insisted on calling it—Marci didn't argue. She did want to look her best tonight.

Because even though she had serious doubts about the future for her and Christopher, Henry was right. Some opportunities only came around once.

And she'd be a fool not to give this one a chance.

* * *

As Christopher ascended the steps to the porch of The Summer House restaurant, high on a bluff on the outskirts of 'Sconset, he tapped in the number his exchange had passed on and took in the sweeping view of the Atlantic.

It was too bad his parents had been delayed at the hotel with a business call—but maybe this would give him a few minutes to get a reading on Marci before they showed up. The quick phone call yesterday finalizing tonight's arrangements hadn't been enlightening. When he'd broached the job, she'd sidestepped the subject.

Maybe he shouldn't have kissed her.

But the magic of the moonlight had chased away common sense.

It hadn't, however, convinced her to give him an answer—and in eleven days a plane would whisk her away if he couldn't convince her to stay.

As he chatted with his patient on the phone, he turned away from the sea and scanned the bar through the bank of tall French windows—homing in on a blonde with fabulous legs in a black cocktail dress.

Marci was already here.

Still talking to his patient, he moved across the porch and stepped inside.

She was angled away from him in the bar area, and he stayed off to the side to finish the call, his mind only half on the conversation as he leaned one shoulder against the wall. His patient's stuffy nose didn't require total concentration. He'd much rather focus on the lovely woman waiting for him.

Apparently the brawny thirty-something guy at the bar felt the same way.

Christopher straightened up as he caught the direction of the man's gaze.

It was aimed at Marci's legs.

The guy picked up his drink, slid off his stool, and ambled over to Marci. His slightly slurred voice carried across the room as he moved in on her. "Hi, gorgeous. Can I buy you a drink?"

Marci turned slightly toward the guy and gave him a quick once-over. "No, thank you. I'm waiting for someone."

"You don't have to wait alone." The dark-haired jerk leered at her and edged closer. Too close. "No one should let a lovely lady cool her heels."

Enough.

Christopher ended the call with uncharacteristic abruptness and strode toward the duo. Marci had no doubt been deflecting passes from men for years—but she didn't have to deal with this guy alone.

As he joined them and took Marci's arm, both turned his direction. While he eased her behind him, he assessed her "admirer." The guy's focus was off, his reflexes slow, and when he took a startled step back his drink sloshed out of his glass as he struggled to keep his balance. The smell of alcohol on his breath was potent.

Christopher gave him a cold, hard stare. "Back off, mister. The lady isn't interested."

"Hey, buddy, I don't want any trouble." The man took another step back and held up a hand, palm forward.

"Good." Christopher kept his own hand firmly on Marci's arm and urged her away from the bar and around a corner. "Sorry about that."

Her smile didn't quite reach her eyes. "No worries. Trust me, I've run into that type before."

"I'm sorry about that too." He directed a dark scowl toward the bar. "This is usually a classy place."

She lifted one shoulder. "It's okay. Blond hair and a decent body seem to attract men like light attracts moths."

Her tone was matter-of-fact, without even the barest hint of conceit. It was as if she'd long ago accepted that her beauty was as much a curse as a blessing.

Understandable, if tonight's episode was a regular occurrence.

"It's *not* okay. And for the record, my interest in you goes way beyond skin-deep."

"Thank you. And thank you for stepping in tonight." She fiddled with the clasp on her purse. "No one's ever done that before."

"Maybe that's because you come across as such a strong person. I'm sure you were more than capable of handling that jerk tonight."

She gave a brief, mirthless laugh. "A drink in the face tends to do the trick."

He arched an eyebrow. "Seriously? You've done that?"

"On rare occasions. But I prefer not to make a scene unless there's no other option." She took a deep breath and tucked her purse under her arm. "Are your parents here?"

He gave the place a sweep over his shoulder. "Not yet. Dad got a call from the office that delayed him. They should be along any minute."

"In that case, I think I'll visit the ladies' room."

"You want me to walk with you?"

"I appreciate the offer—but I'm used to taking care of myself."

Without waiting for a reply, she walked past the lounge area without sparing it a glance.

As she disappeared, Christopher returned to the foyer to wait for his parents, her parting comment replaying in his mind.

Maybe she was used to taking care of herself—but that didn't quash the strong protective instinct tonight's incident had roused in him.

Further proof that his motive for pushing Marci to take the director job was about more than her professional qualifications.

* * *

Marci pulled her comb out of her purse and ran it through her hair, willing her stomach to stop churning. Unless she calmed down, she wouldn't be able to eat a bite of dinner.

Meeting Christopher's parents was nerve-racking enough. She hadn't needed that little interlude in the bar.

But she couldn't hide in the ladies' room all night.

Two minutes later, after a silent pep talk, she worked her way back to the entrance of the restaurant.

She spotted Christopher before he saw her. In his beige slacks, navy blue sport coat, and open-necked white shirt, he looked very preppy—and very handsome.

But it was the two people with him who drew her attention.

A slender woman with reddish-brown hair swept back into a chic chignon stood beside a gray-haired man who fell an inch or two shy of Christopher's height. He, too, wore a sport coat—wheat-colored—with dark slacks and a blue shirt.

As she drew close, the family resemblance was apparent. Christopher had his father's lean build and broad shoulders. From his mother he'd inherited his blue eyes and strong cheekbones.

All at once the older woman turned toward her. Touched Christopher's arm.

As if sensing her trepidation, he came toward her and took her hand in a firm clasp, weaving his fingers with hers. Giving her a reassuring squeeze, he drew her into the circle of his family and made the introductions.

Marci shook hands with Christopher's father and found herself pulled into a hug with his mother.

"Call us Brad and Carol." Christopher's mother spoke in her ear. "We're a low-key, informal bunch."

That might be true, but the understated elegance of her attire reeked of class—and money. You didn't have to be able to afford designer duds to recognize quality in clothes...*or* people.

And Christopher's parents had it in spades.

As she and Christopher followed his parents to their table,

she smoothed down the skirt of her dress. The same black number she'd worn to JC's wedding, bought on sale at Target, and somewhat the worse for wear after her trek through the rain that night.

No way could the polyester frock compare to Carol's silk shantung sheath, which matched the hue of the blue hydrangeas beginning to bloom outside the window. And Carol's discreet but stunning gold and diamond pendant put Marci's cheap faux pearls to shame.

They were shown to a linen-covered table by the window that offered a panoramic view of the sea. As Marci scanned the menu the waiter handed her, she stifled a gasp. A person could eat at Ronnie's for a month on what this dinner for four was going to cost!

"How does that sound, Marci?"

At Christopher's question, she turned to him. "I'm sorry—I was distracted for a minute."

"I'm having that problem myself." At his wink, her heart skipped a beat. "Do you like crab?"

"Yes." Not that she'd ever had the opportunity to eat much of it. High-end seafood wasn't a menu staple at Ronnie's.

"Why don't we start with crab cakes?"

"That's fine."

"Christopher tells us you've just gotten your master's in social work, Marci. Congratulations." Carol's massive diamond engagement ring sparkled as she lifted her glass of water and took a sip.

"Thank you."

"And you came to Nantucket for your brother's wedding?"

"Yes."

"What brought him here?"

"He was a detective in Chicago and took a leave of absence."

Marci closed the menu and set it aside. "A friend of his is the police chief here, so he took what was supposed to be a temporary job as a summer officer. He ended up meeting his future wife, and the rest is history."

"It's odd how you can meet the right person in the most unexpected places, isn't it?" She cast an amused glance at her son.

Marci kept her focus fixed on Carol. "Um...how did *you* two meet?"

Christopher's mother took Brad's hand. "Shall I tell the story, or do you want to?"

"Your storytelling abilities are far superior to mine."

"That's true." A dimple appeared in her cheek as she gave her husband an affectionate nudge. "We were both students at Harvard. Brad was in the law school, and I was in government with my sights set on a diplomatic career in an exotic location. Our paths never crossed on campus, but one summer I did an internship in Paris. Brad happened to be doing a typical student tour of the continent with a few of his buddies, and we ran into each other under the Eiffel Tower, of all places. We started chatting, and realized we were both from Harvard. As you said about your brother, the rest is history."

"Mom and Dad just got back from Paris." Christopher helped himself to a roll. "They celebrated their fortieth anniversary with dinner in the Eiffel Tower."

"And she was as beautiful as the day I married her." Brad covered his wife's hand with his.

The waiter delivered the appetizers, saving Marci from having to reply. Providential, since she had no idea how to respond. There were no student tours of Europe in her world. Nor had there been trips to Paris. Or a Harvard education.

"Did Mark call you today?" Carol directed the question to Christopher when the waiter departed.

"Yes. The whole crew was on the phone with their usual off-key rendition of 'Happy Birthday.' And Eric"—Christopher turned to Marci—"he's my seven-year-old nephew—wanted to tell me all about their trip to Bermuda."

Marci stared at him. "Is today your birthday?"

"Yes—but I'm trying to ignore them these days."

"You're too young to use that line." His father waved the comment aside. "Wait till you're our age. We've heard all about Bermuda too. I'd say the trip was a success."

His brother's family vacationed in Bermuda.

Marci picked at her crab cake. These people went to Europe—and other foreign places—as matter-of-factly as she went to the Loop.

Had she been transported to an alternate universe?

"Say, Christopher, you'll never guess who we had dinner with the other night. He wanted us to pass on his regards."

When the older man mentioned one of the Supreme Court justices, Marci almost choked on the sip of water she'd taken.

"Marci?" Christopher touched her shoulder.

"I'm fine." She coughed out the word.

"Anyway, he's planning an extended trip to Europe during next year's recess. Told me I ought to take a long break too."

"Maybe you should consider it. That would give you and Mom the chance to spend a few weeks in Italy and take that Greek island cruise you've always talked about."

"I may consider it—but it's hard to take extended breaks from a firm with your name on it."

"There are plenty of lawyers there who could pick up the slack." Carol broke off a bite of her crab cake.

Christopher's father owned a law firm.

Any hope she'd harbored about meshing their two worlds

was dwindling as fast as an ice cube in Ronnie's sweltering kitchen. Christopher had never talked about *any* of this!

"Tell us more about your family, Marci."

Praying for inspiration, she took a drink of water. She couldn't lie—but this wasn't the time or place to go into her dysfunctional childhood. "Besides JC, I have one other brother. He's still in Illinois. But we stay in close touch."

She was saved from further explanation by the waiter's return, and Marci used the food-ordering interlude to compile a list of questions that would deflect the attention from her.

As they all handed over their menus, she addressed Christopher's mother. "I've never been to Paris. I'd love to hear more about your trip."

That conversation took them through their salads and up to the delivery of their entrées.

Poking at her seared halibut, Marci searched for another innocuous topic. She'd already gleaned that Carol didn't have a career outside the home, but the dynamic woman across from her would be the type who kept busy with worthwhile causes. A discussion of those should carry them through the entrée portion of the meal.

"So, Carol—do you have any special interests?"

The older woman laughed. "Too many, to hear Brad talk."

"Only because you manage to rope me into all kinds of activities. I'll never forget the year you signed us up to serve Thanksgiving dinner at a homeless shelter and we had to traipse all the way downtown on streets better suited to ice hockey than driving."

"That's true." Christopher flashed his dimple at her. "Mark and I threw our skates in the car just in case."

"But you know what?" Carol played with her fork. "That was one of our best Thanksgivings. The people we served were so grateful—and it made us appreciate our blessings all the more."

"It did indeed." Brad lifted his glass in salute.

"In terms of ongoing activities, though, my volunteer commitment to Birthright means the most to me. I didn't know much about the organization until Christopher joined the board and got me involved. It's such gratifying work. Can you imagine anything more worthwhile than saving the lives of unborn children?"

The crab cake congealed in Marci's stomach. "That's a very commendable activity."

She waved aside the praise. "I only volunteer one day a week. Others do much more. By the way, Christopher, Allison asked me to say hello."

"How's she doing?"

"Great. She's one of the best workers there and has really gotten her act together. Can you believe Sam is almost four?"

"Time slips away, doesn't it? I'm glad her life is more on an even keel."

"Allison was a patient of Christopher's at the clinic," Carol explained.

"What clinic?"

Carol looked at her son. "You haven't told her about the clinic?"

He shifted. "It's no big deal, Mom."

"It is to the people you treated." She redirected her attention to Marci. "He volunteered at this clinic in a, shall we say, less-than-desirable area of Boston. Allison came in asking about an abortion. She'd had one a couple of years before and found herself back in the same situation. Different father. Christopher encouraged her to at least talk to the people at Birthright. Long story short, she decided not only to have the baby, but keep it. As you can imagine, since she speaks from personal experience, she's very effective when talking with young women who are thinking about making a different choice."

"We need more advocates like her." Christopher rested his elbows on the table and linked his fingers. "Think of all the innocent lives we could save if we could help women understand that there are other options for dealing with an unplanned pregnancy besides killing the child."

Marci fisted her hand in her lap. If the knot in her stomach got any tighter, what little food she'd managed to down was going to come back up.

Thank goodness Brad redirected the conversation.

"Tell us the latest on the elder-assistance plan you've been working on."

The conversation during the remainder of the meal focused on Caring Connections. Christopher played up her role and tried to draw her in, but Marci didn't add much. How could she maintain an upbeat front when the fairy-tale dreams she'd allowed herself to indulge in were disintegrating by the minute?

As dinner wound down, Christopher leaned close to her ear. "Are you feeling all right?"

"Yes."

"You didn't eat much."

She surveyed her plate. Most of her entrée was untouched.

"Would you like to take that home, miss?" A waiter paused beside her.

At the prices this place charged, it would be a sin to waste her meal—but did well-bred people take food home from a classy joint like this?

"You're lucky you live here." Carol gave the remains of her meal a rueful survey. "I'd take mine home if I wasn't staying in a hotel."

That cinched it.

"Yes, please." Marci moved aside to let the waiter remove her plate.

No sooner had he whisked away her food than another waiter appeared carrying a cake with flickering candles on top. He set it in front of Christopher.

"Shall we sing?" Brad's lips bowed.

"No. The wake-up call rendition this morning was sufficient, thanks. When did you arrange *this* surprise?"

"Your mother took care of it."

"What's a birthday without a cake?" Carol tapped the edge of the cake plate. "Make a wish."

Marci folded her hands in her lap…and Christopher reached out and covered them with one of his.

His wish was clear in his tender gaze…as was his concern.

He knew something was amiss.

What he didn't realize was that she was on the verge of bolting. She didn't belong here, in this close-knit family circle. Not with her sordid history and a past she couldn't change.

If she followed her instincts and made a hasty exit, though, it would ruin Christopher's birthday. She couldn't do that.

But the instant they finished their cake, she was out of here.

13

Something was very wrong.

As Christopher ate his last bite of cake, he gave Marci a surreptitious scan. She'd downed no more than a few forkfuls of her dessert, mashing the remainder into a small, gooey lump in the middle of her plate. And she'd grown increasingly subdued as the meal progressed.

While it was possible her encounter with the guy in the bar was responsible for the pall that had fallen over her, that didn't ring true.

Could it be a case of meet-the-parents nerves, despite their attempts to put her at ease with their usual charm and grace?

No. That didn't feel right either.

He wadded up his napkin and placed it beside his plate.

Too bad she'd insisted on driving herself tonight. If she'd let him pick her up, the ride back to the main town would have given him an opportunity to try and ferret out the reason for her mood shift.

Since that wasn't possible, he was left with only one alternative.

Marci set her napkin on the table and reached for her purse. "It's been lovely meeting you both." She directed her comment to his parents. "I hope you won't mind if I make it an early evening, but I have a busy day tomorrow."

She rose, and Brad immediately did the same. Christopher wasn't far behind.

"Of course not, my dear." Carol smiled and extended her hand. Marci took it, then shook Brad's.

"I'll walk you to your car." Christopher pushed in his chair.

A flash of panic tightened her features. "That's not necessary."

"Yes, it is." He stepped back and waited for her to precede him. Short of making a scene, he'd left her no option but to go with him—and she'd told him earlier she didn't like scenes.

Shoulders drooping a hair, she eased past him and set a straight path for the door. Once outside, she took off at a fast clip.

But his stride was longer. He moved beside her, taking her arm as they walked down the restaurant path toward the quiet lane on the bluff above the beach where she'd parked. "You want to tell me what's wrong?"

"Nothing's wrong."

"Sorry. Not buying it."

Silence.

"Come on, Marci. Talk to me."

As they approached her car, she fumbled through her purse for her key. "Why didn't you tell me it was your birthday?"

Was *that* what this was all about?

"I didn't want you to feel obligated to get me a present. Your presence at this dinner was gift enough. Is that why you're upset?"

"I'm not upset."

"Marci." He moved in front of her and clasped her upper arms, searching her face in the moonlight as his fingers absorbed her tremors. "I know you're upset. Why won't you tell me what's wrong?"

The faint crash of the sea on the beach below couldn't mask

MEANT FOR EACH OTHER

her soft, sad sigh. "I'm sorry, Christopher, but this thing between us...it's not going to work."

His mouth went dry. "Why not?"

"Our different backgrounds, for one thing. I knew you came from money, but..." She shook her head. "Your parents and brother fly to exotic places as easily as I take the bus downtown. Your dad owns a law firm. A Supreme Court justice is a family friend. Trust me, blue-collar Marci would never fit into your blue-blood family."

"You have as much class as anyone I've ever met. And I don't care about your background. Family pedigree—or lack of one—has nothing to do with how I feel about you."

"I would never fit into your world, Christopher." She dipped her chin, a hint of tears in her voice. "There are probably a dozen socialites waiting for you to come back to Boston. Women who know which fork to use with which course. Who know which side of the Seine is frequented by high-class people. Do yourself a favor. Forget about me and find yourself the right kind of woman."

Christopher filled his lungs with the salt air.

For the first time in their acquaintance she'd given him a glimpse of the insecure woman behind the tough facade she presented to the world. A woman whose trust level with men was as low as the diminutive Brant Point Light because of jerks like the guy in the bar. Whose hardscrabble background made her feel unworthy of mingling with what she considered the upper class.

"Let's talk about this." He tried to twine his fingers with hers, but she pulled away.

"Talking won't change our backgrounds."

"I told you, I don't care about that. And neither do my parents. They're not snobs."

"They also don't know my family history." She tipped up her chin and looked at him. "Did you tell them my father deserted us? That we lived in a tenement? That JC raised us?"

"No." He raked his fingers through his hair. "It never came up."

"It will. And there's a lot more you don't know."

"Such as?"

A few beats of silence ticked by as their gazes locked. When she spoke, the words came out broken, like shells on a beach after a violent storm. "Your mom asked me about my other brother tonight. I evaded the question. You know why? Nathan's in prison for armed robbery."

Christopher took a slow breath as he digested that. "Okay. So you have a black sheep in the family. A lot of families do."

"He's not a black sheep anymore. We reconciled last summer, after being estranged for a dozen years. And when he's released next spring, I intend to do whatever I can to help him get a new start. So an ex-con is going to be part of my life. How do you think your parents will react to that?"

"If we get serious, they'll be supportive."

"How do *you* feel about it?"

"If he's important in your life, he'll be important in mine."

No response.

It was impossible to read her face in the dim light—but she was slipping away. He could feel it.

His lungs began to short-circuit. "Marci, all that matters in the end is how we feel about each other. I still want you to take the Caring Connections director job."

Please, Lord, don't let her turn me down outright.

After a few more beats, the tense line of her shoulders collapsed. "Why don't we let everything rest for a day or two? Once we get Henry home and settled, we can talk again. You may have second thoughts after all this sinks in."

"That's not going to happen."

"Please, Christopher." The plea was tear-laced. "Don't push me tonight. Your parents are waiting for you, and I don't want to spoil your birthday."

Before he could respond, she slipped into the car and pulled the door shut behind her.

He let her drive away—because pressing her tonight could backfire. They were both too emotional.

But tomorrow was another day—and he wasn't giving up without a fight.

* * *

Marci stepped back in the gazebo and inspected her handiwork.

The lace-edged placemats she'd found in Henry's dining room dressed up the café table they'd moved from Edith's guest cottage to the gazebo for the welcome-home dinner. Marjorie's fine china, along with a tiny vase in the center filled with an array of flowers from his garden, added an elegant touch. The yard was pristine. And the dinner she and Heather had prepared at The Devon Rose earlier today—including the chocolate tarts Henry loved—was waiting in his kitchen.

Everything was perfect for Henry's homecoming.

Except the relationship between his two main benefactors.

She moved forward and straightened a fork that was a bit out of alignment.

The radio silence from Christopher since the dinner with his parents two nights ago was hard to interpret. It could mean he'd been extra busy—or it could signal second thoughts.

For both their sakes, the latter would be easier.

Because if he persisted, she'd have to tell him her secret. And from what she'd gathered at his birthday dinner, that would lead to a rejection far more devastating—and deeply personal—than one based on family background.

At the crunch of tires, she rubbed her palms down her festive, floral skirt. There'd be ample time to lament over her own problems later. For now, she'd focus on giving Henry the joyous homecoming he deserved.

Marci hurried across the lawn to the porch and positioned herself for a clear view of Henry's face as he came around the back corner of the house and got his first glimpse of the gazebo.

A car door shut. Then another. The latch was lifted on the gate.

Her heart began to thud.

Fifteen seconds later, Henry rounded the corner—and came to a dead stop. He lifted one hand to his chest. "Oh, my."

The hushed comment, and the glow of joy and wonder that suffused his face, said it all.

Marci looked at Christopher, and for an instant the walls between them dissolved.

Together, they'd brought Henry home again.

And because of Caring Connections, they'd be doing the same for many more people in the future.

Pulling her gaze from his, Marci stepped down from the porch and crossed the lawn to join the two men. "Did we get it right, Henry?"

He turned to her. "The only thing missing is Marjorie. But you know what? I can feel her presence again." He surveyed the yard. "The garden is just like she always kept it, and the gazebo is the same as the original. How did you manage this?"

"We showed Chester Shaw the photo by your kitchen table, and he drew up the plans. He and Christopher and my brother pitched in to build it."

"But it was all Marci's idea," Christopher added.

Henry smiled at her. "You are one special lady, Marci Clay. Would you mind if an old man gave you a hug?"

"Well...I don't see any old men around here—but I'd love to have a hug from you."

She stepped into his thin arms, and he gave her a hearty squeeze. Shifting toward Christopher, Henry stuck out his hand. "Thank you both—for everything."

"Hey, the evening's just getting started." Marci motioned toward the gazebo. "You two gentlemen take your seats and I'll rustle up the first course."

When she returned with a tray of salads, Henry was settled into his place at the table.

"You know, I wasn't real sure I'd ever see this view again." He shook out his napkin as she put his salad in front of him.

"I told you all along you'd come home." Marci finished serving the salads and slid into her seat.

"I guess the good Lord was watching out for me. I think a little prayer of thanks is in order." He bowed his head.

Christopher did likewise.

Marci followed their lead, even if praying before meals wasn't part of her routine. But if ever there was a day to be thankful, this was it.

"Lord, we thank you for this meal shared with friends. For eyes to see and ears to hear the beauty of your sea and sky and flowers. For restored health and hope for tomorrow. Thank you, too, for sending these two special people into my life when I needed them most. Please bless them, as you blessed me, with a love that transcends time—and help them recognize it when they see it. Amen."

In her peripheral vision, Marci could see Christopher watching her. He had to be wondering why she wasn't open to exploring the relationship everyone else in their acquaintance was pushing them toward.

Thankfully, he didn't bring up the subject during the dinner. Neither did Henry. The conversation was lighthearted, and Henry's stories about his early years on Nantucket kept them entertained throughout the homecoming dinner.

As dessert wound down, however, it was clear he was tiring. A cue Christopher picked up as well.

Setting his coffee cup back in its saucer, he smiled at Henry. "I don't know about you, but I'm about ready to call it a night."

"At seven o'clock?"

"It's been a long day."

"For me, maybe. I suspect you have a bit of life in you yet. Why don't you walk me in and then come back and enjoy my new gazebo with this pretty lady?" He winked at Marci.

Subtlety was *not* Henry's strong suit.

Cheeks warming, Marci rose and began stacking their dessert plates. "If you want to get Henry settled, I'll start the cleanup."

Christopher scooted his chair back and stood. "Okay—but I'll be out in a few minutes to follow through on Henry's suggestion."

"That's my boy." Grinning at Christopher, Henry leaned on his arm as he got to his feet. Then he reached out and squeezed her hand. "Thank you again."

Pressure built in her throat. "It was my pleasure, Henry."

She watched as the two men slowly crossed the yard, one tall and strong in body, the other a bit stooped and strong only in spirit. Yet they were both men of integrity and deep moral fiber, whose hearts beat with the same kindness and caring and decency. And they both considered her special.

But they were wrong. She was flawed. And tainted. And sinful. She'd made bad mistakes, and though the passage of years had diminished their power to keep her awake at night, it hadn't reduced their magnitude. Nor, much to her regret, had time helped her find a way to rectify them.

Spirits nosediving, she loaded the tray with dishes and hefted it up. As she'd done year after year at Ronnie's while pursuing her degree and clinging to the dream of a better life.

She had the degree now—and when she got home, she'd find a job far away from Ronnie's.

That dream had come true.

But the long-suppressed dream Christopher had reawakened probably wouldn't.

Because he wasn't going to let the evening end without finishing the discussion they'd tabled the night of his birthday.

Meaning she was going to have to tell him about her past.

And it wasn't going to be pretty.

* * *

"Stop fussing, Christopher. I'm fine. Trust me, I'll sleep far better in my own bed than I ever did at that assisted-living place with all those old folks. You go back out there and keep Marci company."

Christopher picked up the medical alert button on the nightstand. "Remember this is here. And promise me you'll keep it with you whenever you're at home. That's part of the deal."

He scowled at the device. "Thanks to Patricia."

"I happen to agree with your daughter on this point. It's a prudent safety measure. If you'd had one with you when you fell, you could have called for help."

He sighed. "I guess it's a small price to pay for independence."

"Keep that in mind. And welcome home, my friend."

"Thank you. I'm happy to be here. Now get out there and smooth-talk Marci into taking the job with Caring Connections."

"I'll do my best."

After closing the door behind him, Christopher followed the sound of silverware against china to the kitchen. He'd honored Marci's wishes to defer the discussion about them until Henry was home, but she was leaving in nine days. He couldn't wait any longer.

"Need a hand?" He strolled into the room and snagged a dish towel from the rack

"There isn't much left to do." She dug into the suds in the sink. "We prepared everything at The Devon Rose, and I already cleaned the carrying containers and put them in my car. I'm almost finished with the china and glassware."

He picked up a plate with a delicate gold rim and an off-white embossed filigree pattern around the edge. "Did you see Henry's face light up when he realized you'd used Marjorie's china?"

Her lips curved up. "Yes."

"You made his homecoming special."

"I'm just glad he *could* come home." She twisted the faucet off, wiped her hands on a towel, and picked up the plate Christopher had dried. "I'll put these away in the dining room."

She made several trips back and forth, and as she returned

from her last one, Christopher was laying aside his dish towel.

"Chester said he'd come over Friday and pick up the table and chairs." Marci wiped down the counter and hung the dish rag over the faucet. "I thought Henry might want to put one of the wicker rockers from the back porch in the gazebo, with the little side table."

"I'll take care of it this weekend."

"Thanks."

She picked up her purse, and he frowned. "You aren't leaving, are you?"

"The party's over."

"Not according to Henry."

"He never gives up, does he?"

"No. That's a huge factor in why he was able to come home." Christopher propped a shoulder against the wall and folded his arms. "It's also one of the attributes he and I share."

Her knuckles whitened on the edge of her purse, and she let out a shaky breath. "I was hoping you'd realize our different backgrounds were a problem and let this go. That would have been easier."

"What does that mean?"

"There are other reasons why this won't work."

The cold finality of her tone left a hollow in the pit of his stomach. "Why don't we go out to the gazebo and talk about them?"

Maintaining her grip on her purse, she walked to the door, her gait stilted.

He followed her across the yard in silence. She sat on the edge of the raised platform—the same place she'd occupied when he'd asked her to take the job.

That did *not* send positive vibes, given the outcome that day.

Steeling himself, he sat beside her and rested his forearms on his knees. Waited.

She scanned the sea, its surface placid in the early evening. But the ocean around Nantucket was deceptive. Beneath the calm veneer, riptides and strong currents seethed, roiling the waters.

A metaphor for the woman beside him, based on her shallow breathing and the film of sweat above her upper lip.

"I told you about my upbringing." Her words were soft. Sad. "My family was dirt poor and dysfunctional. After my father left and my mom died, we were even poorer. If it hadn't been for JC, I don't know where Nathan and I would have ended up."

She plucked a single sky-blue petal from the blooming hydrangea beside her. Cradled it in her hand. "JC tried his best to keep Nathan and me on the straight and narrow. He could never reach Nathan, but for a while I believed what he told me—that if I worked hard I could improve my lot. So I did. And it paid off. I got a scholarship to college. The day that letter came was one of the proudest of my life."

She stopped, and Christopher bit back the question hovering on the tip of his tongue. He had to let her tell this story in her own way, at her own pace.

Marci traced the edge of the fragile petal. "Freshman year was amazing. I made excellent grades, and for the first time in my life I began to believe I had more to offer than a great body. Then I met Preston Harris III." She lifted her hand. A few seconds later the wind snatched the petal from her palm and flung it to the ground.

He picked it up. Pressed it back into her cold palm. "Always hold tight to beauty."

Her throat worked, and she curled her fingers around the petal as she continued. "Pres was a big man on campus. Good-looking, football jock, wealthy family. He noticed me for the same reason men always notice me. But he seemed different than the rest. His gifts and invitations didn't come with strings or expectations. He was the kind of man I'd always dreamed of finding. A true gentleman. I fell in love." A tear welled on her lower lash. Spilled over.

Christopher lifted a hand to brush it away, but she jerked back.

"Don't." Her voice was raw as she swiped at the moisture. "I won't get through th-this if you touch me again."

She was poised to bolt.

He lifted his palms. "Hands off. Promise."

She took a shuddering breath. "After a while, he said he loved me too. That we'd get married when we finished school. But in the meantime, he wanted to take our relationship to the next level." She examined the petal in her hand, already beginning to shrivel from the heat. "I knew it was wrong. JC had drummed that into me from the day I turned thirteen. But then Pres began to suggest I was using him. Taking all his gifts and dinners without ever intending to follow through. In hindsight, I realized he was manipulating me—but back then, I thought it was important to prove to him my love was true. So I...I gave in."

She dropped the withering petal to the ground again. "I'll spare you all the gory details. But a month later, I overheard Pres talking to one of his buddies about me. And discovered he'd never had any intention of marrying me. I was just a 'cute chick to have some fun with,' as he told his friend."

Christopher clenched his teeth. Flexed his fingers. If Preston Harris III was standing here right now, he'd get an earful—plus a faceful of fist.

"I'm sorry for everything you went through, Marci. But

you're not the first woman to be taken in by a smooth talker. It doesn't change how I feel about you."

"There's more." She swallowed, drawing attention to the staccato pulse beating in the hollow of her throat.

He braced.

Bad as her story had been so far, the worst was yet to come.

"I was devastated. And angry—at him and myself. I broke it off immediately and resolved never again to let anyone use me. I was also determined to move on, to consider the mistake tuition in the school of experience. And then I...I found out I was pregnant."

Christopher stopped breathing.

"When I told Pres, he suggested the b-baby wasn't his. That he'd always been 'careful.' And he went on to say that someone like me must have 'gotten around,' as he put it, so the father could be anyone." Her voice broke, and she sucked in a lungful of air. "But I hadn't. In fact, he was my first real boyfriend."

Marci stood, crushing the discarded blue petal beneath her foot as she put distance between them and folded her arms tight against her chest, angling toward the sea. "I didn't know what to do. I couldn't tell JC. I didn't want him to be disappointed in me. So I talked to Nathan. He gave me some money that was probably stolen and advised me to get rid of the b-baby."

Shock rippling through him, Christopher stood too—but remained by the gazebo.

"I didn't want t-to do it. But I couldn't see any other option. The responsibility of a baby freaked me out. I had no way to support a child. So I had an abortion, thinking that would solve my problems. Instead, that's when they really s-started."

Another tear trailed down her cheek, but she seemed oblivious to it.

"I thought I could handle the guilt—but I was wrong. It tore me up inside. I dropped out of school. Drifted from city to city, working odd jobs to eke out a living, sampling the drug scene, searching for an escape, running from what I'd done. That was how I lived for five years—until finally I couldn't run anymore. Couldn't deal with the emptiness."

She swallowed. Massaged her temple. "In the end, I came home. Got a job at Ronnie's Diner. Went back to school. To all appearances, I had my act together at last." She bowed her head, and when she continued Christopher had to strain to hear her muted words. "But you know what? The regrets never went away. To this day, I still have dreams about the baby who never had a chance to live—because of me."

Christopher grasped the gazebo upright beside him. Held on tight as his world tilted.

Being misled by a smooth-talking campus hotshot was one thing. But killing the most innocent of life? The type of baby he'd worked so hard to save through Birthright?

No wonder Marci hadn't wanted to share this secret. She knew it could be a deal-breaker.

Was it?

He wiped a hand down his face. If he wanted this relationship to have a chance, he should pull her into his arms. Tell her that her past didn't matter to their future.

But it did.

How could he reconcile her actions with everything he believed?

Seconds ticked by as he grappled with that dilemma.

Too many.

Marci turned toward him, the abject misery and despair in her eyes ripping at his gut.

He searched for words. Came up empty.

"I have to go." She darted toward the gazebo, snatched up her purse, and ran across the yard.

He started to follow. Stopped.

Less than a minute later, her car engine roared to life. Receded into the distance.

Quiet descended in Henry's garden, save for the muted boom of the surf that sounded like a distant, ominous rumble of thunder. The kind that signaled an approaching storm destined to wreak devastation and send sensible people scurrying to find shelter and safety.

People like him.

But he didn't feel sensible right now. All he felt was alone.

And unless he wanted to feel that way for the rest of his life, he'd have to find a way to make peace with Marci's past.

A monumental task that could take a miracle to pull off.

14

Someone was banging on her door.

Groaning, Marci rolled onto her back and squinted at her watch. Eight-thirty a.m. Meaning she'd gotten all of two hours of sleep, since tears had kept her awake until dawn.

"Marci! Are you in there?"

It was JC.

She groaned again.

Could she ignore him?

He knocked harder.

Apparently not.

"Hang on a minute." She swung her legs to the floor, shoved her hair back, and padded to the door.

JC gave her a once-over. "Did I wake you?"

She tried to smother a yawn. "Yeah."

"Sorry. I figured eight-thirty was safe. I seem to recall you telling me not long ago that only slugs slept this late."

"And as you reminded me, sleeping late on vacation is an exception to that rule. I'm supposed to rest and relax, right?"

"Yeah—except you don't do much of either, as far as I can tell." He planted his fists on his hips and scrutinized her with that shrewd detective eye of his. "As a matter of fact, you don't look too hot."

"Gee, thanks for the ego boost. And the purpose of this visit is?"

"Ornery today, aren't we?"

She mashed her lips together.

"Fine. I get the hint. This came for you yesterday." He handed over an envelope with an Illinois postmark.

Nathan.

He'd been writing to her every week in care of The Devon Rose.

"I also wanted to remind you about having dinner with Heather and me on the beach before the fireworks." JC propped his hands on his hips.

She fingered the envelope. Too bad she'd accepted his invitation for the Fourth of July festivities. After last night's conversation with Christopher, she was in no mood to celebrate.

"You know...I appreciate the invite, but I think I'll pass."

One side of his mouth hitched up. "Better offer?"

"No."

"Wasn't your doctor friend at the welcome-home dinner for Henry last night?"

"Yes." She edged the door closed.

"I'm surprised he didn't suggest getting together for the holiday."

Why prolong this? He'd find out the truth eventually.

"I doubt I'll be seeing him anymore, JC."

Her brother's brow puckered. "Why not? I got the distinct impression he was interested in you. Edith thought so too."

"We're not a good match."

"Why not?"

"We're too different. I had dinner with him and his parents a few nights ago. They're Boston high society. His father owns a law firm. They jet all over the world. Need I say more?"

His jaw hardened—just as it had years ago when she'd come

home from school one day crying after classmates made fun of her threadbare, thrift-store coat. "Did they snub you?"

"No. They went out of their way to put me at ease. But they live in a different world, JC. I wouldn't fit in."

He studied her in silence for a moment. "You don't think you're good enough for people like the Morgans, do you? Well, you know what? That's garbage. You're every bit as good as they are. You overcame tremendous odds to get where you are. It's a testament to your character that you succeeded." He raked his fingers through his hair and expelled a breath. "Why can't I convince you of that?"

"Trust me, JC. It wasn't meant to be."

A muscle ticced in his jaw. "Maybe I'll go have a little talk with Christopher."

"No! Don't you dare! It's *my* life. *My* decision."

Several beats of silence ticked by as he scrutinized her. "I'm picking up strange vibes here. Why do I have a feeling you aren't telling me everything?"

"Because you're naturally suspicious. It must go with the detective badge. I want you to promise me you'll leave this alone." When he clamped his jaw shut, she got in his face. Or as close as possible, given his height advantage. "Promise me, JC."

Several beats passed before he heaved an exasperated sigh and backed down. "You are one stubborn woman, you know that?"

"Is that a promise?"

"Yeah, yeah."

"Good. Now go home to Heather. Enjoy your day while I clock a few more Zs."

"The invitation is still open if you change your mind about joining us later."

"Thanks."

After she closed the door, Marci wandered back to the bed. If it had been difficult to drift off in the early dawn, despite her exhaustion, she'd never succeed in broad daylight.

Using her scrunched-up pillows as a backrest, she sat cross-legged on the bed, Nathan's letter in hand.

But her mind was on Christopher—as was her heart.

Which was foolish.

Allowing herself to believe he might be able to live with her history had been nothing but a pipe dream. The truth was, she could never escape her past. It was part of who she was, and it always would be.

Perhaps if she'd met an accountant or an engineer—or someone who didn't have such a strong faith—the outcome could have been different.

But no. She'd fallen for a doctor. A man committed to healing the sick and saving the unborn, whose faith was the guiding force in his life.

And that was depressing.

Because if Christopher was the kind of man who attracted her, the verdict was in—his kind of man would never want anything to do with her kind of woman.

She hugged Nathan's letter to her chest. At least she'd repaired her relationship with *him*. If nothing else, her brothers would always be there for her. Heather too. JC's wife treated her like a sister.

Pushing thoughts of Christopher aside, she tore open the envelope, withdrew the single sheet of paper, and scanned the note.

Hey, Sis. Hope this reaches you by Fourth of July. I can't wait to celebrate my own independence day in ten months and fourteen days. (Can you tell I'm counting?)

I had a letter from JC last week. He mentioned you were dating a doctor on the island. That brightened my day. Until our talks during your visits over the past year, I never realized how my bad advice twelve years ago had affected your life. I've been praying about that, seeking forgiveness for my role in your problems. And I'm beginning to find release from the guilt.

I know you feel guilty too, and I wanted to encourage you to give it to God, like I finally did. Let him forgive you—and then forgive yourself. Even though none of us can change the past, I've come to believe that it's possible to build a better tomorrow.

If this doctor is important to you, please don't blow him off without giving God a chance to touch his heart—and yours. Take care of yourself...and stay in touch.

Love, Nathan

Slowly Marci refolded the letter.

It would be wonderful to find the forgiveness Nathan spoke of. To let go of the pain and anguish that still had the power to twist her stomach into knots. But she'd never felt worthy enough to even *ask* God for forgiveness.

Yet Nathan had done bad things too—and he'd made peace with his past.

Could she do the same?

Maybe.

The service she'd attended with Christopher had been a positive experience. In that small church, she'd felt the presence of the Almighty—and a pervading hope.

Why not go again?

She stood and tucked Nathan's letter into her purse.

Edith had mentioned a holiday service this morning at nine. It was too late for that—but she could slip into the church afterward for a private visit.

And maybe—just maybe—God would give a prodigal daughter the guidance and comfort she desperately needed.

* * *

The aroma of fresh-brewed coffee greeted Christopher as he stepped onto Henry's back porch, and he inhaled the caffeine-laced scent. A cup of java was exactly what he needed after his sleepless night—along with a shower and shave.

But Henry was top priority.

Before he reached the door, the older man pushed it open. "Good morning. I saw you crossing the yard." He gave him an assessing perusal. "Grab a cup of coffee and we'll sit a spell in the gazebo. You look like you could use a jolt of caffeine."

"Sold." Christopher crossed the kitchen and pulled a mug from one of the hooks under the cabinet. "But I can't say the same about you. You seem very perky this morning."

"Haven't slept that well since before I fell. Nothing like being in your own bed. Hospitals and assisted-living joints aren't very restful."

"True." Christopher filled his mug and rejoined Henry by the door. "Take hold of my arm while we cross the yard."

"I'm not an invalid."

"And I want to keep it that way. You're recovering from major surgery. No one's as steady as usual after an operation. I want you to be extra cautious for another couple of weeks."

His neighbor took his arm. "You're a smooth talker, you know that?"

Christopher's gut clenched. "Not always."

The older man squinted at him. "I'm not liking the sound of that. You aren't going to tell me you couldn't convince Marci to stay, are you?"

They'd arrived at the gazebo, and Christopher helped Henry step up to the platform. He waited to respond until they were both seated at the café table. "I didn't try too hard."

The older man cocked his head. "That doesn't sound like you. Why not?"

Christopher took a sip of coffee. Maybe the caffeine would clear the cobwebs from his brain. "She gave me a number of reasons last night why she didn't think we had a future."

"Good reasons?"

"Maybe."

"Hmph." Henry pursed his lips. "Family differences?"

"She brought those up, but I told her they didn't matter. It was the other reasons she shared that gave me pause."

"Interesting." Henry weighed his mug in his hand. "Why do you think she did that if she thought they were a deal-breaker?"

Not a question he'd considered.

"Because it was the honest course, I suppose."

"Indeed it was. Seems to me that shows a boatload of integrity—and courage." Henry took a slow sip of coffee. "When you love someone, you try to protect them. Do what's best for them—even if that isn't always in your own best interest."

"No one ever said anything about love."

"Not in words. But anyone who's ever loved can recognize it in someone else—and I've been seeing plenty of it right here in my own backyard." He set his mug on the table and leaned forward. "Marci didn't have to tell you her secrets, yet she chose to let you see the whole package before you got too involved—despite the risk of losing you."

Christopher wrapped his fingers around his mug and stared into the dark liquid.

Henry was right.

Marci's feelings ran as strong and deep as his. They were there for the world to see, reflected in her eyes.

As was her breaking heart when she'd turned toward him after he'd rejected her.

And that's what his silence in the aftermath of her revelation had been—as loud and clear as if he'd spoken the words.

A wave of nausea swept over him.

He didn't want to hurt Marci. She'd been hurt too much already in her life.

He wanted to love her.

But how was he supposed to deal with her past?

"I don't know what she told you last night, Christopher, but I can see it's got you tied up in knots." Henry laid a hand on his shoulder. "Must have been a powerful story. You in the mood to hear another one?"

A curious nuance in Henry's tone managed to penetrate the clutter in his brain. "Sure."

Settling back in his chair, Henry took a measured sip of his coffee and surveyed the horizon, where a distant boat churned purposefully forward, maintaining a steady course. "You know about my service in Korea."

"Some. You've never given me much detail."

"That's because most of it was ugly. I told you once a lot of the guys I served with were haunted by the memories for the rest of their lives. I didn't tell you why. But I think it's time you knew."

Henry set his mug on the table and folded his hands over his stomach. "Korea was a bad place, Christopher. Most of the

American foot soldiers were young, undertrained, underequipped, and unprepared. We were dealing with an aggressive enemy, plus a huge refugee population that the North Korean soldiers often mingled with—in disguise. After they got behind American lines, they'd conduct guerrilla operations. As you can imagine, it was a tense situation, and we were always watching our backs." Henry gazed again toward the sea, his features contorting. Almost as if he was in physical pain.

"You don't have to tell me this, Henry."

"Yes, I do. For Marci's sake."

Christopher frowned. "What does your experience in Korea have to do with Marci?"

"You'll see in a few minutes. I hope." Henry took a deep breath. "We'd been told to consider refugees hostile and to keep them off the roads. We'd also been told to search them whenever they crossed our path. One day a dozen or more approached. We called to them to halt. They didn't. We tried again. Same result. There were only a few of us on that patrol, and we were nervous. The day before several of our buddies had been killed or wounded by enemy soldiers who'd infiltrated a group like the one we were facing."

Christopher leaned closer as Henry swallowed and picked up his coffee. His neighbor's hand was trembling as he took a sip and carefully set the mug back on the table.

"As they drew closer, one of them reached inside their coat. I panicked and pulled the trigger. Chaos erupted. More shots were fired. The refugees scattered, what was left of them. Eight were killed by me and my fellow soldiers. Five were women. Two were old men. One was a child. The person I shot was a woman. I thought she'd been reaching inside her coat for a weapon. But when I opened it, I found a baby. Also dead."

In the silence following Henry's story, Christopher tried to imagine the stomach-churning horror of that moment.

Failed.

Nor could he reconcile the frail, tender-hearted older man beside him with the terrified young soldier who'd pulled the trigger that spawned a massacre.

Yet they were one and the same.

"I never told that story to anyone except Marjorie, Christopher. And I almost didn't tell it to her. I was ashamed, and I thought she'd reject me if she knew what I'd done. But in the end, I couldn't in good conscience ask her to marry me without letting her see into my soul, with all its dark places. I had to take that risk. It was the right thing to do."

"What did she say?"

The whisper of a smile softened Henry's features. "She took my hand, looked me in the eye, and said, 'You were young, Henry—and afraid. You were trying to protect yourself in a hostile environment. Yes, you made a tragic mistake. But in your heart, I see only kindness and caring and empathy. I know you would never hurt anyone out of malice or anger. Your spirit is too gentle. That's why I love you. And that will never change. So make your peace with the Lord and then let it go—as I intend to.'"

Christopher leaned back. "She must have been a remarkable woman."

"She was—and I'm sharing morning coffee with a remarkable man."

"Not even close."

Marjorie had looked into Henry's heart and recognized that only extraordinary circumstances would have caused him to act in such an uncharacteristic manner.

He hadn't done the same for Marci, even though she'd been

young and afraid, ill-equipped and unprepared for the challenge she'd faced too. Like Henry, she'd panicked and cut short a life.

Unlike Marjorie, he'd remained silent—and inflicted untold hurt...and damage.

He set his elbows on the table and dropped his head into his hands. "I really blew it, didn't I?"

"It's not too late to make amends."

"It might be." Despite the rising sun, the world suddenly felt bleak as a gray winter day on Nantucket.

"Nope. Marci will give you another chance. That's the kind of woman she is. Some people go through fire and get burned so badly their scars never heal. Others are forged by fire. I don't know what Marci told you, what bad experiences she had or bad decisions she made. But I do know she has a kind and forgiving heart." He took a sip from his mug. "I know one other thing too. Whether she's ready to admit it or not, she loves you. And love changes everything."

A rallying cry if ever he'd heard one.

Christopher picked up his mug and stood. "I think I'll take a drive into town. Would you like me to help you inside before I leave?"

"No. I'm going to stay here and reminisce—but I want a full report later."

"Wish me luck."

"Goes without saying." Henry lifted his mug in salute. "But you do your part too. Letting that little lady get away would be foolish—and you're no fool, my friend."

Maybe not.

But he'd acted like one with Marci.

And as he strode across the lawn toward his cottage, he could only hope she'd be as generous and forgiving as Henry expected.

Even if he didn't deserve it.

* * *

"Well, this is a surprise!"

At the sound of Edith's voice, Marci twisted toward the door of the church. Her landlords were crossing the lawn, aiming for the bench she'd claimed.

"Hi, Edith. Chester."

The older man gave her a shy smile.

"What brings you to church today?" Edith adjusted the oversized purse on her shoulder.

"Just paying a visit. I was too late for the service, so I decided to wait out here until it was over."

"You could have come in. God doesn't give out tardy slips." The older woman chuckled at her own quip. "But you go right on in now. The place will be cleared out in a matter of minutes. Everyone has holiday plans. See you later."

She commandeered Chester's arm and towed him toward their car.

Marci waited five more minutes, then slipped inside the empty church, choosing a pew near the back.

For a long while she sat there, letting the peaceful ambiance soothe her, but finally she pulled the guide for today's service from the rack on the pew in front of her and began paging through it.

A quote from Ephesians jumped off the page at her.

"I pray that the eyes of your heart may be enlightened, so that you will know what is the hope of his calling."

How odd.

It was as if JC or Nathan were talking to her. Both of her brothers were always praying she'd see the light.

The imagery of the passage was spot-on too. For the heart

did see. Often more clearly than the eye. As for finding hope in the call of the Lord—that had happened with Nathan last year...and his life had been transformed.

Maybe it was her turn now. Better late than never, right? After all, Edith had just told her that God didn't give out tardy slips.

Marci took a deep breath. What could it hurt to try? Worst case, God would reject her—and she was used to that.

Folding her hands, she bowed her head.

Lord, you don't know me very well, but my brothers are friends of yours. You've probably heard them mention my name a few hundred times. Sorry about that. They can be annoyingly persistent.

And then she laid it all out. The mistakes. The guilt. Her regrets. Her dilemma with Christopher. And her desire to be loved by someone who was kind and caring and decent and generous. Someone like Christopher.

If you could show me how to—

"Marci?"

She jerked and twisted her head.

Christopher stood in the aisle, dressed in khaki slacks and a blue dress shirt. But he wasn't his usual put-together self. He'd missed one of his buttons, his hair was damp and a bit tousled from a very recent shower, and he'd nicked his chin shaving.

"May I join you?" He motioned toward the pew.

She slid over. Given the smudges beneath his lower lashes and the lines of strain around his mouth, he hadn't slept much, either.

"What are you doing here?" She clenched her hands in her lap.

"Looking for you. I stopped by the cottage, and Edith told me where you were. I'm glad I ran into her. I would never have thought to check here."

Of course not.

Her lips crimped. "Yeah. Marci Clay in a church. Imagine that. I'm surprised God hasn't tossed me out on my ear."

Twin furrows dented his brow. "That's not what I meant."

"Maybe not—but it's true."

"God welcomes everyone, Marci—even people who make mistakes. Like me."

What?

"You haven't made any mistakes that I've noticed."

"I made a big one last night when I let you walk away."

Her heart did a quickstep—but she ruthlessly smothered the tiny ember of hope that ignited. She'd indulged in romantic fantasies about Christopher once. She wouldn't set herself up like that again.

"You did the right thing. You deserve better than me."

"Marci." He angled toward her and took her hands in a tender grip. "Give yourself more credit than that. You're a very special woman. You're smart and caring and funny and strong and kind. You have a generous, loving heart. And you've added an incredible spark to my life. I should have said all that last night, and I'm sorry I didn't. My only excuse is that you walked away before I could process everything you told me."

She tried to think, but the warmth of his fingers was short-circuiting her brain. "I did dump a lot on you."

"That's true—but I've had all night to think about it. And here's where I stand. I know our relationship is new, and I'm not suggesting we rush this. What I'd like you to do is stay and take the director job with Caring Connections. Give me a chance to court you. And put the rest in God's hands, see where he leads us. What do you say?"

"Why do you want me, after all the mistakes I made?"

Somehow she choked out the question.

"Everyone makes mistakes. That doesn't mean we're bad people. It just means we used bad judgment. All we can do is learn from them and move on." He stroked his thumb along the back of her hand, creating a trail of fire. "As Henry reminded me this morning, I'd be a fool to let you go. I agree. So please…say you'll stay."

Hope bubbled up in her heart. Spilled over. "Is this for real? You honestly want me, after everything I told you?"

"Yes. So will you stay?"

All she could manage was a nod.

"Then come with me." He stood and tugged her to her feet.

"Where are we going?" She didn't resist as he led her down the aisle and out the front door, into the dazzling sun of a glorious Nantucket morning.

In silence, he guided her to the side of the porch, behind the privacy of a tall hydrangea bush laden with blossoms, and pulled her into his arms. "To seal our bargain."

Before she could respond, he gave her a kiss that communicated more eloquently than words the joy and love that was in his heart.

When at last he released her lips, he settled his hands at her waist. "What are your plans for the rest of the day?"

"I don't have any."

"You do now. Ending with fireworks."

"I just had my fireworks." She traced his lips with a whisper stroke of her finger.

His eyes darkened. "How about an encore?"

Once more, his mouth settled over hers in a kiss that spoke of promises and hope and a new tomorrow.

In other words, it was a dream come true.

For Christopher's love hadn't simply filled her world with joy. It had also liberated her from the shadows of her past.

And it was a gift she would treasure every day of her life—just as she would always treasure the special man who'd given her an Independence Day to remember.

Epilogue

As Marci drove toward 'Sconset in the deepening dusk, a contented smile curved her lips. It was hard to believe how fairytalelike her life had become in the past five months. It was like the Cinderella story—except her ball hadn't ended at midnight.

Caring Connections was up and running, and public reception and support had been phenomenal.

Her job as director gave her everything she'd ever hoped to find in a career—satisfaction, joy, and the gratification of knowing she was doing meaningful work that made a difference in people's lives.

JC and Heather were close by, and in five months Nathan would join them to complete their original family circle.

She'd made new friends like Edith and Chester and Henry—whom she was visiting today.

And then there was Christopher.

As large, lazy flakes of snow began to fall, adding a pristine topping to the already white world, she gave a contented sigh.

Month by month, their relationship had deepened and flourished. If ever she'd harbored doubts about their ability to reconcile their different backgrounds, they'd vanished. Christopher had made it clear in every word and every action that he valued her for who she was. All her old baggage had been relegated to the basement—where it belonged.

Life didn't get any better than this.

Marci turned onto Henry's lane and eased the car to a stop in front of his cottage. A cranberry wreath hung on the front door, and golden light spilled from the windows. Visible through the panes was the tree she and Christopher had helped him decorate last weekend in anticipation of the holiday. Although Patricia had invited him to spend Christmas in Boston, he'd chosen to stay in his snug cottage and celebrate the day at The Devon Rose with Marci's family, joined by Christopher and Edith and Chester.

After setting the brake, Marci slid from behind the wheel and rounded the hood, the snow crunching under her boots. Though it wasn't windy, the air was cold. But the scarf she'd wrapped around her neck, plus her gloves and earmuffs, should keep her toasty.

As she approached the front door, she squinted at a note taped above the bell.

"Knob's being cranky. Come around back."

Odd. The knob had been working two days ago.

Switching direction, Marci strolled toward the gate that led to the backyard. Fortunately, there was a retired carpenter in 'Sconset on her Caring Connections resource list. She'd have to send him over tomorrow to check it out.

As she covered the short distance to the arbor, she scanned the ground. Someone had shoveled the narrow path. Hopefully not Henry. He'd been doing great, but another fall could set him back.

Pushing through the gate, she blinked a snowflake off her eyelash and lifted her face to the heavens. A few stars were beginning to twinkle in the distance where the sky was clearing, while above her lazy flakes continued to sift down from the indigo expanse.

It was so quiet and peaceful. Only the muted sound of the surf broke the stillness.

Until the hushed strains of "I'll Be Home For Christmas" suddenly drifted through the quiet air from the back of Henry's cottage.

Why was music playing in the backyard?

She picked up her pace—but came to an abrupt halt as she rounded the corner and took in a scene that was pure magic.

Outlined with glowing white twinkle lights and bedecked with boughs of greenery and large red bows, Henry's gazebo had been transformed into an enchanting winter wonderland.

And waiting for her inside was the man of her dreams.

Dressed in jeans and a fleece-lined suede coat, he gave her a smile that warmed her to her core despite the frosty air.

She continued forward, stopping at the edge of the structure. "Hi."

"Hi." The husky tenor of his voice sent her pulse tripping into double time.

"Did you do this?" She swept a hand over the gazebo.

"I did the work. Henry supervised."

"Why?"

He held out his hand, and when she took it, he tugged her up beside him. "Because this gazebo represents love—and I couldn't think of a more appropriate place to propose."

Propose?

Now?

Of course she'd known they were heading this direction—but the timing was sooner than she'd expected.

Before she could gather her thoughts, Christopher cradled both her hands in his. "I know we said we'd take this slow—but we've known each other for seven months. And I've never been more sure about anything. I want to spend the rest of my life with you, Marci. If you prefer to wait a while to get married, I can live with that—as long as I can put a date on the calendar. In ink."

Backing up a step, he urged her into one of the wicker chairs that had taken up residence in the gazebo. Then he dropped to one knee in front of her and took her hand in his. "Marci Clay, I love you with all my heart, and I promise you I always will. For better or worse, in good times and bad. Just like these Christmas lights have illuminated Henry's gazebo, you add light to my life every day of the year. Will you do me the honor of becoming my wife?"

Joy overflowed in Marci's heart, and with a hand that wasn't quite steady, she touched his face. "Yes." Her response came out in a whispered cloud of frosty breath.

He exhaled. Closed his eyes. "Thank you, Lord."

"You didn't think I'd say no, did you?"

"A man never knows for sure until he hears the word." He stood and pulled her to her feet. "I think we should warm up our lips, don't you?"

She gave him a teasing grin. "Are you serving hot chocolate?"

"Maybe later. I had a faster method in mind." He pulled her into his arms, a dimple denting his cheek. "I have to warn you. We probably have an audience."

"I don't mind if you don't. Henry played a major role in bringing about this happy ending."

"He also has a vested interest in the outcome."

"How so?"

"He and I had a long talk while we decorated the gazebo. He said his cottage is getting too big for him, and he offered to sell it to me—or, I should say, to us—and move next door to the guest cottage. But there was one caveat. We have to give him unlimited access to the garden and gazebo. What do you think?"

She grinned. "He drives a hard bargain—but caveat accepted."

"Then why don't we set his mind at ease?"

She wrapped her arms around his neck and tugged him close, until their faces were only a whisper apart. "Let's."

He bent down to seal their engagement in the most traditional of ways while the melodic words of the carol drifted through the night air.

I'll be home for Christmas, if only in my dreams.

And as she lost herself in the magic of his kiss, Marci gave thanks. For here, in Christopher's arms, her dreams had come true.

She was home.

For always.

Keep reading for a preview of Book 4!

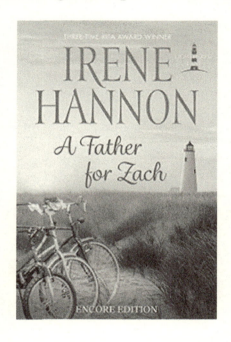

~Excerpt~
A Father for Zach
LIGHTHOUSE LANE—BOOK 4
ENCORE EDITION

1

Nathan Clay gazed out over the sparkling blue waters off Nantucket, scanned the pristine white beach, and took a long, slow breath.

What a change from the tiny, windowless cell he'd left behind four days ago—his home for the past ten long years.

The juxtaposition was surreal.

Settling back in the white folding chair, he tugged at the tie that was cutting off his air supply, surveyed the seventy-five wedding guests assembled on the lush, garden-rimmed lawn that abutted the beach, and tried not to feel out of place.

It was a losing battle.

What were the odds anyone else in this high-class group had served time in prison? Certainly not the Supreme Court justice on the other side of the aisle, who was a longtime friend of the Morgan family.

The family his sister, Marci, would be marrying into in just a few minutes.

Talk about moving up in the world.

But she deserved it. Marci had worked hard to build a better life. To rise above their tough upbringing.

Too bad he hadn't done the same.

Then again, his childhood had been even rougher than hers—or his big brother's.

All because of the secret that had darkened his life for more years than he cared to recall.

He swallowed past the sudden, bitter taste on his tongue. Sucked in a lungful of the cleansing, salty air. Suppressed the ugly memories.

Those days were history. They couldn't hurt him unless he let them. And never again would he give his past that kind of power.

A string quartet positioned to his right began to play, and he focused on the measured, calming cadence of the classical music as he surveyed the four musicians. Attired in black dresses, they blended together perfectly, each handling her instrument with a confidence that spoke of long hours of practice.

Especially the violinist.

Eyes closed, she swayed slightly as she drew the bow back and forth over the strings, producing pure, clear notes that quivered with emotion.

The little he knew about music wouldn't fill one of the clamshells he'd found while walking on the beach yesterday—but he did know about losing yourself in art. That had been his salvation during his decade behind bars.

And this woman was lost in hers, the sweep of her long lashes feathering into a graceful arc against her cheeks as she wielded the bow with graceful elegance.

He continued to study her as guests arrived for the ceremony.

A FATHER FOR ZACH Excerpt

Although her light brown hair was secured at her nape with a barrette, wispy bangs softened the no-nonsense style. The early afternoon sun highlighted her classic bone structure and warmed her flawless complexion, while the whisper of a smile played at her lips.

His gaze lingered on their supple fullness...and all at once it became even *more* difficult to breathe.

Running a finger around his too-tight collar, he forced himself to turn away—and found his new landlady, Edith Shaw, observing him from two rows back. When their gazes connected, she winked.

What did *that* mean?

Not a question he could dwell on, because the music changed and an expectant hush fell over the guests as the ceremony began.

The minister, groom, and best man took their places beside the wooden gazebo where the vows would be exchanged, and Nathan angled in his seat to watch his sister-in-law walk down the aisle as matron of honor. Heather was as radiant as a bride herself—perhaps due to the pronounced baby bump that heralded the arrival of a new generation of Clays.

As the music changed again and Marci appeared on JC's arm, Nathan focused on his sister. She'd always been beautiful, but today she was luminous as she slowly made her way toward the gazebo—and the man she would soon promise to love and cherish all the days of her life.

She smiled at him as she approached, her wispy veil drifting behind her in the gentle May breeze, her hand tucked in JC's. It was fitting their older brother should walk her down the aisle. He'd stood by both of them through the tough times, believing in them when neither had believed in themselves.

When they reached his seat, Marci paused and grasped his hand. "I'm glad you're here, Nathan."

At her soft words, he blinked to clear his vision. "So am I."

With a gentle squeeze, she moved on to take her place beside the tall physician who had claimed her heart. As they joined hands beneath swags of white tulle held in place by sprays of pale pink roses and feathery fern, Nathan gave thanks that she'd found her happily-ever-after.

Perhaps someday, God willing, he could do the same.

His escort duties finished, JC joined him in the first row. Nathan shifted over to give his older brother a bit more room—and take another peek at the violinist. She was angled sideways now, and over her shoulder Nathan caught a glimpse of a little blond-haired boy sitting behind her on a white folding chair.

Her son?

He zoomed in on her left hand, where a glint of gold in the early afternoon sun satisfied his curiosity.

She was married.

More disappointing than it should be—but not a surprise. She appeared to be in her thirties, and most women that age had found their significant other.

Not that it mattered. The odds of connecting with the first woman to catch his eye were minuscule at best.

But maybe...just maybe...there was a woman out there somewhere who would be able to overlook his past. Who would delve into his heart and see that it had been transformed.

"I, Marci, take you, Christopher..."

As his sister's vow echoed strong and sure in the still air, Nathan shifted his attention back to the weathered gazebo. Marci stood framed in the lattice archway, chin tipped up, her gaze locked on the man she loved as she repeated the phrases after the minister.

Today she would begin a new life.

And so would he.

For better rather than for worse.

* * *

An hour later, a piece of cake in one hand and a glass of punch in the other, Nathan stepped into the garden of The Devon Rose. An appropriate spot for the wedding reception, since Heather's Lighthouse Lane tearoom was where fate had set Marci's courtship in motion.

Once more, the genteel music of a string quartet drew his attention, and he wove through the crowd, following one of the brick paths that crisscrossed the formal garden with geometric precision.

When the ensemble came into view, he stepped off to one side. It was the same group that had played at the wedding. The musicians must have packed up their instruments and come straight to the reception the instant the ceremony ended.

The little blond boy was here too, tucked into a nook a few feet away from his mom, who was shooting him frequent, protective glances. He was sitting on a folding chair, swinging his dangling legs, not in the least interested in the book lying in his lap. Instead, he was eyeing the plates of cake being juggled by the guests who were milling about.

Lips quirking, Nathan navigated through the crowd to the child and held out his untouched plate. "Would you like a piece of cake?"

The little boy's demeanor brightened, but he hesitated and cast a silent plea toward his mother.

Nathan angled toward her—and at her narrow-eyed perusal, his stomach knotted. Those kinds of looks had been part of his life for as long as he could remember—but he'd hoped he'd left them behind.

Shifting his weight from one foot to the other, he waited for her decision.

Finally, without missing a beat of the music she was playing, she gave a slight nod.

"Oh, boy!"

At the youngster's enthusiastic reaction, Nathan swiveled back to him and handed over the plate. "I had a feeling you liked cake."

The boy dived in, spearing a hunk of frosting with the fork. "I like the icing best." He proved it by putting the whole glob in his mouth at once. "Than koo."

Nathan lifted his cup of punch in acknowledgement. "You're welcome. Enjoy it."

He started to walk away, but the boy's voice brought him to a halt.

"My name's Zach. What's yours?"

A quick look confirmed that the violinist's jade-green irises were fixed on him. Watchful. Warning him off. Her tense posture was a direct contrast to the soothing classical music emanating from her violin.

Instead of moving back toward the youngster, Nathan responded from where he stood. "Nathan."

"You want to see my book?" Zach held up a Dr. Seuss classic.

"I don't think your mom would like that."

Zach's face fell and he lowered the book to his lap. "Yeah. I guess not." He poked at his cake. "The only good thing about weddings is the cake."

"Do you go to a lot of weddings?"

"Uh-huh. They're all the same. B-o-r-i-n-g."

In his peripheral vision, Nathan caught the boy's mother watching him.

Too bad.

Sitting still for such an extended period with no one to talk to had to be torture for a youngster. A bit of pleasant conversation would have helped him pass the time.

But in light of the strong back-off vibes his mother was sending, Zach was in this alone for the duration.

At least it couldn't be personal. She'd seemed protective at the wedding too—and here as well, even before he'd spoken to Zach.

Why?

A question likely to remain unanswered.

Nathan stayed where he was. "Hang in there, champ. It'll be over before you know it."

"That's what Mom always says." The boy heaved a resigned sigh and continued to shovel cake into his mouth.

"She's right. It will still be daytime when this party is over. Maybe you can play with your friends later."

"I don't have any friends."

Before Nathan could follow up on that unexpected response, the song ended and the little boy's mother spoke in a quiet but insistent voice.

"Zach, come over here and let me wipe that sticky icing off your fingers or it will get all over your jacket."

The youngster speared the last bite of cake and shoved it into his mouth. After scooting off his chair, he trotted over to his benefactor with the empty plate. "Thank you. That was good."

"You're welcome."

Plate in hand, Nathan lingered as the boy joined his mother. But when she gave him another suspicious scan and pulled her son close while she fished a tissue out of her purse, he took the hint—and took his leave.

Still wondering why the precocious little blond-haired boy had no friends—and why the green-eyed beauty was so wary.

About the Author

© DeWeesePhotography.com

Irene Hannon is the bestselling, award-winning author of more than sixty contemporary romance and romantic suspense novels. She is also a three-time winner of the RITA Award—the "Oscar" of romance fiction—from Romance Writers of America, and a member of that organization's elite Hall of Fame.

Her many other awards include National Readers' Choice, Daphne du Maurier, Retailers' Choice, Booksellers' Best, Carol, and Reviewer's Choice from *RT Book Reviews* magazine, which also honored her with a Career Achievement Award for her entire body of work. In addition, she is a two-time Christy Award finalist.

Millions of copies of her books have been sold worldwide, and her novels have been translated into multiple languages.

Irene, who holds a BA in psychology and an MA in

journalism, juggled two careers for many years until she gave up her executive corporate communications position with a Fortune 500 company to write full-time. She is happy to say she has no regrets.

A trained vocalist, Irene has sung the leading role in numerous community musical theater productions and is a soloist at her church. She and her husband enjoy traveling, hiking, Saturday mornings at their favorite coffee shop, and spending time with family. They make their home in Missouri.

More information about Irene and her books can be found at www.irenehannon.com. She loves to interact with readers on Facebook, and is also active on Twitter and Instagram.

Made in the USA
Coppell, TX
03 April 2024

30879637R00132